Fiona Cooper was born in Bristol in 1955 and has lived in London since 1973. She has been writing 'ever since I was knee-high to a dingbat', with short stories published in *Cosmopolitan*, in *Passion Fruit* (Pandora Press), and *Woman's Day* in Australia. Her first novel, *Rotary Spokes*, was published by Brilliance Books in autumn 1988. She is currently working on 'the definitive novel about unrequited love and a coffee-table extravaganza on performance drag'.

Heartbreak on the High Sierra is a lesbian western in true spaghetti tradition, bubbling with thrills, spills and suspense; a story that begins with a cataclysmic storm and builds up to a rip-roaring climax, a romance where love and laughter reign supreme, and all the baddies bite the dust.

D0912557

HEARTBREAK ON THE HIGH SIERRA

FIONA COOPER

Published by VIRAGO PRESS Limited 1989
20–23 Mandela Street, Camden Town, London NW1 0HQ

Copyright © Fiona Cooper 1989

A CIP catalogue record of this book is
available from the British Library

Printed in Great Britain by
Cox + Wyman Ltd, Reading, Berkshire

This book is dedicated, with love, to
Barbara Britton

Acknowledgements and thanks to: Sue O'Sullivan, Sara Maitland, Reg Bundy, Susan Forrester, Kate Rae-Scott, Genia Goelz, Annabelle Reynolds, Julia Darling, Tenebris Light, Neil McKenna.
Thanks also for inspiration: Mae West, Lanie Kazan, Marlene Dietrich, Madeline Kahn, Patsy Cline, Cloris Leachman, Ellie-May Clampett, Calamity Jane, and all lady outlaws everywhere.

ONE

I had given up on riding as the path contoured upwards in switchback swirls. I only knew the mare was somewhere behind me in the wind-wrung darkness, when the reins near snapped my hand in two as she tugged and shied against the stygian gloom and mud torrent. I'd have left her behind, but for the weighty saddlebags bearing everything I owned in this life. This was no road for a good animal.

The blizzard sprang at me out of the dark like a mottled leopard streaks from hiding; centuries of meat-lusting muscle drove against me; chill claws raked my face and body. This pussycat was ravenous for blood.

I knew it would be best to stop, make camp, rest until the morning. But when the hell did I ever do what was best? All the milestones of my life mark moments I've taken the sinister fork, plunged down the nearest rocky gulch when a grassy sunlit path was mine for the taking. Some folks are born with a foot on the path to heaven, some are plain hellbent, Mom had told me years before. *Follow yer dark star, daughter of Satan!* she had shrilled when she found me and the hired girl having us some fun in the hayloft. Whatever you say, Mom. That night I left my home, setting my compass by that dark star. And I've been travelling on for more years than I care to recall.

I knew if I could just get through the demon white blasting my eyes and face, there would be respite, shelter from the storm on the other side of the pass. It was hours since I'd rested, reining in by a broken farm on the plain behind me. Hospitality was grudging, had been for some three days. At this bleached-out no-hope end-of-line building, it took some time for the folks to mosey out and stare. Four of them: an old greybeard, shrunk and leathery like a saddle been ridden hard for many a year; a younger man, still big and muscled, face baked to brick in the unforgiving wind and sun of the plain; a work-aged woman, face grey with hours toiling over a slow range in a dark cabin; a boy with hair and skin pale as oatstraw, growth-shooting bony wrists and dirt-streaked feet below faded shirtsleeves and cut-down men's Levis. Homesteaders that paid their dues in sweat and blood for a thin living eked out from the grudging land.

'Sheeee-it! Yurr a woman,' cackled the greybeard. 'We in't needin' no hired help.'

'I ain't offering none,' I drawled, sliding from my saddle. 'Jest a little water for m' horse.'

'I'll put on some coffee,' said the grey-faced woman like she was preparing for a funeral. We straggled into the pinch-penny kitchen.

'So whar y'all headin', stranger?' said her husband, with a look that would bake bread to french toast.

'Thru' the pass,' I said.

A ripple went through the dismal quartet, like sparks along damp fuse wire, and fizzled out at the greybeard's ravaged features.

'Whut in the hail yah want theah?' he demanded.

'They say th' air's clean,' I said evenly.

'Whut about th' company?' said the woman, pouring coffee. 'Ain't no Christian folk west a here till yuh hit th' coast. They say.'

'I ain't religious.'

Greybeard and Oatstraw conferred in what was intended to be whispering.

'Yuh think she's with that Lorraine woman and her crew?'

'Don't look hard enough, Pops.'

'Whut else they say?' I asked as Momma hushed them.

'There's stories,' she wittered. 'Idle gossip most like . . .' But her weary grey eyes flickered along the path, where even now the jagged mountain range took predatory bites of shadow out of the plain.

2

'They say,' said her man, 'say there's wild people beyond the pass. Wild wimmin! Cayn-ee-bals!'

'Cannibals?' I said, like it was everyday. Wild women I figured I could handle.

'Ain't nobody ben thru' that pass ever come back this way breathin',' said Poppa excitedly. 'Either it's murderers that way, else it's cayn-ee-bals. Gotta be one or th' other. Stories we heard makes it worse en Injuns. Only a month back, we had a corpse tied back uv a palomino come trottin' down th' trail.'

'Poppa!' protested the woman. 'No call t' alarm this young lady. Maybe all th' folks we seen thru' here just went right on tuh th' West Coast. Like we woulda done iffen the wagon hadn't broke and me started with Otis heah.'

Oatstraw hadn't been so far wrong, after all. Otis Oatstraw glared at both parents. It was a tired quarrel. One I didn't have time for. No-hopers full to bitterness with 'iffen this' and 'iffen that'. A weary litany they could chant all their lives. And *iffen* they weren't born losers, then, goddammit, they'd a bin winners. And if I wasn't broke I'd have had money. And so on.

I took my leave.

'We kin fix y' a baid in th' loft,' said the woman, as I cinched my girth comfortably tight.

'Thank yuh, ma'am. No. Best be movin'.'

Her eyes raked the horripilant scars of the mountain range ahead, slashing into the purple-grey clouds beyond.

'There's a storm a-brewin',' she fretted.

'I've been thru' storms,' I told her, swinging myself into the saddle. 'So long, sweetheart.'

I left her blushing – probably for the first time since before she was married. I hate unhappy faces. Especially worn by women.

TWO

I fell back as the reins jerked my arm near out of its socket. Hit a spine of rocks on the way and slid down the pitted mud-chute path, fetching up with a soul-bruising thud against the horse's heaving side where she had stumbled and bit the dust.

'Easy,' I hollered, more to myself than to the shuddering mare – my voice was ripped to silence in the dervish swirls of snow. I crawled along to the frightened head, and patted her neck with hands stunned in the enveloping chill. Suddenly, I had one of those flashes, when cold and pain ease off to give you a break, and you float a little down the warm and sure river of extinction. Maybe this one I wouldn't get through. Better just to lie still by the terrified animal and let myself drift with the numbness.

But the mare flung her head up and let out a shrill whinny, and all at once I was back with a grinding pain burning through my neck where I had been wrenched backwards; the deafening snowbound wind slapping my face sideways with icy pellets like bullets. Alive, and goddammit, against the odds, wishing to stay that way.

'I ain't through yet!' I screamed. I coaxed the mare to her feet, and started up the path again, this time clinging to her sodden mane – to guide her? To guide me? Satan himself would have seen nothing clear through this storm.

Three lifetimes later, somewhere below me, my knees jarred anguish as the path dipped down. Down! We'd done it! Me and the mare were on the other side of the pass. Wind hurled up at us from an invisible icy canyon, and we stumbled downwards, blind, me groping a foot ahead with frozen giant-numb hands.

And then the wind stopped. The blizzard became eerie snowflakes, dropping pretty as petals. Silence thundered loud in my crackling ears, and my body registered sparks of warmth all knotted up with the pistol-whipping I'd just taken from the naked fists of the storm.

My hands hit a rock face and I padded them across more rock – up and down, every which way. Upwards, stretching so my shoulders screamed, the rock shelved out over my head. This would do fine until the sun rose and let me know what kind of place I'd come to. I led the mare against the rock and scrubbed at her soaking coat with my gloves, unstrapped the slippery saddle and bags and dropped them on the unseen ground. The mare trembled and lay down. I collapsed against her. Morning couldn't be too far away.

Near or far I don't know. I woke as the mare heaved upright, snorting.

'Easy,' I muttered, deafened by the sound of my own voice. I opened my eyes. Five feet from my head stood three pairs of boots to be reckoned with: one glossy black leather with shining spurs; one battered and scarred, metal toecaps shifting the dust like a nervous cayuse; one in ancient snakeskin patched over and over. I looked up at three silhouettes against the ice-blue sky.

'*Wild wimmin! Cayn-ee-bals!*'

The old greybeard's voice thrummed in my head like a rusty guitar string. I sat up slowly. Looking at the three figures in front of me, he could have been right.

I have been around some bad ones, avoided most of the worst and what I haven't seen I've heard about. But this trio beat the band for lowlife. Tough? Mean? Those words were too pretty for women like these. At best, they might have risen to *mean* for a special occasion like their mother's funeral. I thought of the corpse tied to the palomino and driven back through the pass: that would be everyday business for women like these.

The one with the shiny black boots had the face of an angel till you looked twice. Blue eyes held a shifting core

5

of hellfire. A full mouth set against high cheekbones, lips stretched into what would have been a smile but for a twist like you make for spitting. There was a white thread of scar tissue on her neck, a gold silk bandanna knotted tight above the burnished collarbone. There down, she was the full dude from her silver-buttoned waistcoat to tooled leather belt, and bleached Levis taut on hard thighs. She had a two-bore trained on me, held very still and glinting in the cold early morning light. A lean streak of pure danger a mile high, with pale gold hair like a halo. But a halo would have sat as well on Lucifer, the proudest of the fallen.

Beside her, a shorter woman, almost squat by comparison. The one with the edgy metal toecaps. Studs on every seam and pocket on her back. Her hair was black and coiled like snakes over thick shoulders. Shirtsleeves rolled high over forearms ridged with muscles like a seashore at low tide; one square hand grasping the butt of a well-used Colt whose blind mouth was staring me right between the eyes. The other hand clenched and unclenched at her side.

The last of the hellish trio had all the Mexican colour and flame of the squat woman, but drawn out over a taller frame to look stylish. Patched boots, Levis crazy-paved with multicoloured patches, a vivid oriflamme shirt. One lean hand was twirling a dagger like a lady of leisure might twist a cocktail stick in a fancy saloon back East. The bright blade twinkled and dazzled me.

'Whaddya want here?' spat the first.

'Yeah, whaddya *want*?' echoed the squat woman, adding low menace to the words.

The third just stared and whirled her dagger to a silver blur.

'On yer feet, boy,' she said.

'Boy I ain't,' I drawled, rising real slow, with my hands away from my body. These three were trigger-twitchy and would need no excuse to shoot, stab or stiletto anything that crossed their path and didn't take their fancy.

6

'Whuh?' The squat woman, twitching.

'Raise yer hands high!' barked the blonde. 'So yer a woman. I asked yuh a question. Whaddya want here?'

I didn't aim to tell them much. That split second of doubt in all six savage eyes told me something. Muscle and murder they might be from head to toe, but these were just three goons couldn't act without a leader. I guessed they had licence to amuse themselves with any male intruder – but for me, they'd have to go back to their boss for further instructions. Were they with *Lorraine's crew*, the name whispered between Greybeard and Oatstraw with such terror? Lorraine? I aimed to meet this suzeraine, and my mind raced around how to get to her with my heart still a going concern.

'I come up thru' the pass,' I said, speaking slow and calm like you do to psychopaths. 'Had enough of the cities and towns and just kept movin' west. I heard there might be a way a woman could live and breathe out here without a wedding band and petticoats to make her decent.'

'Yeah?' A challenge from the stiletto-spinner.

'Yeah,' I said.

They looked at each other. Drew off a little and muttered, without shifting either gun a millimetre from a direct line to my heart and brains.

'Trouble!' said the squat woman.

'Shaddap, Grievous. We oughtta get her back to the bunkhouse. Ask some questions?' The blonde's sky-blue eyes glittered.

'And have Suzanna git mad again?' snarled the tall dark woman. 'We better get her up to the house. That's what she said last time.'

'Naw. We kin sort it out here and now,' said the blood-hungry blonde. 'Lessee what she's got in the bags.'

'Suzanna won't like it,' said Stiletto.

The blonde stepped forward. 'Whuchuh got in the bags?'

'Jest a few things,' I said, ignoring the twin mouths of

7

death hovering over my midriff. Suzanna? Lorraine? Was there more than one gang of wild women here? A rival outfit? Had Suzanna taken over from Lorraine?

The blonde jerked her head at Stiletto. 'Cover her,' she said. 'And git her gun.'

I stood while wiry hands ran over my body like tarantulas. I don't carry a gun but I figured on saying nothing. They would have checked anyway.

The blonde patted my mare. The first sign of human feelings. She bent and unbuckled the saddlebag.

'What the hell is this – a jewellery case?' she sneered. 'You got a pile of rocks in here, or what the fuck?'

'It's my typewriter,' I said without looking.

'Open it. Real slow,' said Stiletto.

I squatted and opened the case. They squatted beside me, and I felt a snub-nosed pistol in my ribs.

'Whassit do?' said the short woman.

'Fuckin' ignorant bitch,' burst in the blonde. 'Show her!'

I got the thickly wrapped pack of paper from the saddlebags and pulled out a sheet.

'It writes,' I said, keeping my voice neutral. I wound the paper in. 'What's your name?'

'Grievous,' snapped the squat woman, jerking the pistol against me. 'I know my own name.'

I typed G.R.I.E.V.O.U.S. Each key hit the page with the sound of a gun-shot echo.

'There you are,' I said and handed her the paper. 'Grievous.'

'Zat so? My name, huh?' She looked at it every which way, then stuffed it in her pocket.

'We ain't much for book-learnin' out here,' said Stiletto.

'You want me to do yours?'

'My name's my own,' she spat.

'And you worked for it, sugar,' crowed Grievous. 'She done mine. It's like a tattoo, only on paper. Her name's Mercedes Assassina.'

'Shut your damn mouth!' snarled Mercedes, turning on her.

'Angel Star,' said the blonde intensely, touching the machine. It pleased her, this new toy: the flinty psychotic gaze had melted to wide-eyed wonder.

I typed again, and added a row of stars. She smiled like a half-wit kid with an ice-cream cone.

'So enough of this bullshit,' raged Mercedes Assassina. 'Do mine. Fast. And let's get outta here. Suzanna'll be waiting.'

She tore the paper from my hand with a cruel curve of the lips.

We had another altercation before we left the high bleak dip of land. My mare was beat. Two days' rest and she'd be fine. If I rode her now I'd be digging her grave by sundown. Assassina was in a minority of one to shoot her here and now. So I wound up riding behind Grievous, Angel leading my horse, and Mercedes Assassina prancing ahead, her stiletto gleaming where she'd stuck it in her thick hair like a jewel.

THREE

The valley lay ahead, green foothills curving like a woman's naked thigh to the plain. Above, peaks rising in great curtains of rock – golden, scarlet, rose, bleak grey hanging along the baby-blue sky. Sheer bluffs strung with silver where the sun danced off ice-cold streams and snow-ermined ridges.

The place was heaven on earth and spoke to some deep need in my wandering soul. My nightmare journey had been the only way to get here and with die-hard vigilantes like my new companions I could see how rumours had fired the curiosity of the deadbeat homesteaders I'd seen the day before. These women wanted no one else on their land and so far they'd done a fine job keeping it that way.

The grass grew thick and lush as we got to the plain, and a herd of horses looked up and galloped away, palomino manes pure light against the sun. The heat made me sleepy and I closed my eyes, jogging against the wall of muscle Grievous wore across her back. Mercedes's spurs jangled as she wheeled back to join us.

'Asleep?'

'Feels like it,' said Grievous. I let myself slump gradually and keyed into the terse staccato of their unguarded conversation.

'Suzanna likes new faces,' said Grievous.

'As you know,' taunted Assassina.

'Your damn mouth runs on wheels,' snarled Angel.

'Come on,' said Grievous. 'You wanna get sore at Suzanna, Angel, you might as well shoot yerself through the foot, give yerself an easy life.'

'There's more to think about than a broken heart,' said Angel. 'If I'd had a heart to break in the first place. I just say, what use is it to have another mouth around the place and one that don't even carry a gun?'

'Relax, Angel, yer makin' me nervous,' said Grievous, and, true, I could feel her heart race. 'We got the pass sewn up where we found this baby, but it's the west we gotta keep an eye out for.'

'I don't like it,' said Assassina. 'Years Suzanna's been here – and never had nothin' come from the west. Who was that guy here the other week? Suzanna said, Don't shoot, I wanna *talk* to him.'

'Talk!' said Angel with a violent curse. 'All evening they spent talkin'. Grits had her ear to the door the whole time and couldn't get a word of sense outta it. Suzanna's gone all high-falutin'. Don't never come down to the bunkhouse since.'

'Years here ain't shit,' said Grievous. 'I spent two in a cell with Suzanna when yuh wasn't even the evil glint in yurr daddy's eyes. The woman got ambition. Yuh can bet your irreligious asses if she's *talkin'* to that guy from the west, she's got plans. Any of her plans ever done yuh harm so far?'

'You want an answer, Grievous?' Angel was cold. 'And don't give me this *I done my time* shit: we all done time.'

'And some of us got sprung mighty quick, Angel,' said Assassina with pure malevolence. 'Five lousy years I sat in Pulque. Three times I been raised at dawn to meet my last sunrise. Three times I got the blindfold and then, no reason I know, back to the cell. You sat on your sweet butt for five months, Angel – five *months*! That ain't nothin'!'

'Aw, stop this shit,' said Grievous. 'I done time, Angel done time, why the hell yuh think we had to come so far away? But I'm tellin' yuh, if it wasn't for Suzanna, yuh'd be drawin' a pension from your cells, both of yuh! And me too. 'Sides, it was me and Suzanna got yuh out, Mercedes. It took for ever! What yuh done *cost*, honey, cost a lot of bucks to winkle yuh outta that cell.'

'Yeah,' said Mercedes. 'Always been handy with a blade.'

It was something she was mighty proud of, but before I could hear the rest of her bragging, there was the sound of hoofbeats ahead, and I made a show of waking up. Three figures emerged from the dust cloud and reined in by us.

'What the hell's this?' said one, jerking a gloved thumb at me. The red in her hair had nothing to do with its dark roots and when she smiled there was a flash of gold.

'Lemme perform the introductions,' said Grievous, more easy than I'd known her so far. 'Hell, what'd you say your name was?'

'I didn't.'

But Grievous had pulled her typed name from her pocket and handed it to the red-headed woman.

'That's my name. She done it on a – whassit?'

'Typewriter.'

'Yeah,' said Grievous. 'My name. Grievous. Typewriter.'

The red-headed woman laughed.

'Grievous, you done good,' she said. 'How'd ya manage to stop these two playing target practice? Huh?'

Assassina and Angel looked sulky. The red-headed woman was older than them and treated both like untrained puppies. Her fellow riders were older, too: the next watch for the pass?

'Lucille,' she said to me, offering her hand with a courtesy that seemed bizarre after the conversation I'd been silent witness to. 'Roo, Mira, looks like we have us another mouth to feed.'

Roo was wiry and small with a mane of grey-streaked curls, and brown eyes that saw right through you. Mira nodded my way.

'Depends on Suzanna, Lucille,' she said in a deep foreign drawl. 'I won't say welcome to you, my friend, until you've seen Suzanna. I don't like brief encounters.'

'Damn! That's good,' said Roo, with a brittle laugh. 'Goes for me too.'

'We better get up to the pass,' said Lucille. 'You have any problems, stranger? Aside from these two – ' Another jerk of the thumb at Assassina and Angel.

'I talked with some folks on the other side. Seem to think there's some cannibals up here. Wild women and cannibals.' I was aware of six pairs of eyes fixed on me.

Lucille flung back her head and laughed. 'You're OK,' she said. 'Giddup there!'

The three rode off. Grievous acted better for the exchange, and even Assassina was calmer, seemed to have forgotten the conversation before, which had felt to me like the lead-up to serious damage or death. Angel talked to my horse.

'That's three a the rest of us,' said Grievous. 'Lariat Lucille – she's one of the neatest things you'll ever see ropin'. Damn! And Mira – shoot a fly off the end a yah nose and never wake yuh! Used to be a trick rider in one of them travellin' shows till the boss got frisky.'

'Roo?' I said.

'Used to be in the same show. Knife-throwin' and fire-eatin'. She and Mira lit out together. Long time back.'

Mercedes and Angel were ahead of us now, and Grievous muttered so only I could hear, 'Yuh was never in any danger, Typewriter. I'm the only one can handle them 'cept Suzanna. They only been here five minutes. They'll learn.'

FOUR

'I'll see to the horse,' said Angel, as a low cabin came into sight. She wheeled away from us.

'Still can't get her ass up to the big house,' jeered Assassina.

'Mercedes, you got a bitch for a tongue,' snapped Grievous. 'Have some respect. A woman has feelings, only I guess you wouldn't know about that.' There was a new assurance in her manner that reduced Assassina to muttered curses.

The path rose now, zigzagging through rocks and trees, and as the trees grew thicker, Grievous slowed a little.

'I'll do the talkin', Typewriter,' she said. 'Suzanna needs respect, I'm warnin' yuh. One word wrong and – forget it.' She drew one finger across her throat.

The trees thinned out on a wide pasture, edged with gleaming sycamores. Their gold leaves were vivid against shaggy-maned oaks in deep purple green. A breeze played over the silver-haired grass, and hectic orange flowers bobbed side by side with snow-white daisies. And the backdrop to this rich tapestry was a two-storied bleach-board house, with a porch running the length of the front. There was a figure on a rocking chair on the porch – a little old lady with thick grey hair and a woollen shawl even in the rising heat of the day. It all looked real homey, till we were close enough to see the heavy twelve-bore across the little old lady's knees, the pitcher of moonshine at her feet, and catch the rip of smoke from a foul yellow stogie glued to her turkey lips.

'Hey, Grievous, Mercedes! Who's this?'

The voice came out with a deep cough and stream of tobacco juice. Many years of rotgut had burned down that scraggy throat to build a sound so rusty and gruff. Was this Suzanna? The old bird was meaner than a one-eyed rattler and sharper than a buzzard's talon. Her eyes raked my face from dusty red pouches of wrinkles.

'Found her near dead up by the pass,' said Grievous.

'*Near* dead? My heart's delighted you kept the brake on this one,' said the old lady, waving a finger at Mercedes Assassina. 'I'll git Suzanna.'

'No need to shift yourself, Fingerbone.'

The voice fell sure and warm as afternoon sunshine. We all looked upwards.

'Suzanna!' yelled Grievous. 'Hot damn! We got company.'

Suzanna stood on the upper balcony, looking down. Even from the ground I was aware of smokey-blue eyes like the glaze on fine porcelain, and a pantherlike power as she placed both hands on the handrail. Then she was completely still beyond a sardonic mouth working a thin dark cheroot. Sunlight splashed on her pale-honey hair like that's all it was made to do. She was a vision in cream rawhide. Double doors were flung wide behind her, with white cotton drapes shifting in the breeze. She might have been on a stage.

'Come on in,' she drawled, and swept out of sight.

I heard firm footsteps on the upper floor and the weighty jingle of spurs as high-gloss chestnut boots came down the stairs. Somewhere before I felt I'd watched this same slow assured walk – but where? Her boots were followed by a lean and restless body, clothed in smooth golden skin. She smelt of clean cotton, leather, expensive smoke and a perfume like walking through a young forest in the heat of the day. Her eyes were electric close to, and energy sparked off her with every movement. I was all at once aware of my travel-wrecked clothes and an aching weariness.

'Sit down,' she said graciously, then hollered, 'Grits! Coffee.'

'I'll make coffee, Suzanna,' said the old woman from the porch.

'When I want to drink hog's piss, Fingerbone, I'll let you know,' said Suzanna. 'You get out to your chair, old lady, and keep a weather eye. And mind yourself lighting them skunk-hide smokes of yours. One of these days you'll set yourself on fire just breathing.'

The old woman shuffled out. Suzanna laughed.

'Mary Maloof Fingerbone, what in the hell did I ever do to deserve her? They broke the fucking mould to make that one.'

She offered me a cheroot. Lit it for me. Sized me up over the flame, eye to eye and no blinking. She tossed a cheroot to Grievous, then swept her eyes to Assassina, with a slight flicker of amusement.

'You been good?' she said mockingly, and I tensed against the fury sure to burst from Mercedes. But there was a iron note in Suzanna's voice. I searched my mind for where I'd heard that before: rich syllables flowing out like a whiplash in slow motion. Mercedes tossed her head.

'Yeah, I been good,' she muttered, finally smiling under Suzanna's powerful stare. Suzanna tossed her a cheroot, and, in a flash, Mercedes skewered the tip of it on her stiletto.

'Good,' said Suzanna. 'That I like. Now git along to the bunkhouse and rest yourself. I need to talk to Grievous.'

Assassina left the room with a shade of a flounce, but quelled.

'What about Angel?' said Suzanna, her steel gaze cutting a path to Grievous, who shrugged.

'Suzanna, the pair of them been twitchy as mosquitoes all night. I heard a horse, they heard a thousand, jumping around and bragging crazy all night long. For chrissakes, Suzanna, I ain't a fuckin' guardian angel. Began to wish some dude would come through so they could plug him and relax a little.'

Suzanna nodded as another woman came in from the kitchen with coffee set out on a gilt-edged tray. Suzanna lived well; fragrant steam hit my nose and I became aware of a growl of hunger deep inside me.

'Drink your coffee,' she said to me. 'You're all beat. That pass is a motherfucking son of a bitch this time of the year. Most times of the year. Grits'll fix us some food – you stayin', Grievous?'

'I'll do that, Suzanna.'

'You better get washed up,' said Suzanna.

Grievous almost tiptoed across the floor and up the stairs, leaving me alone with the woman they'd spoken about with such high feeling on the path. Power was indelibly stamped into every inch of her easy frame. She lit another cheroot, striking the match against the sole of her boot. Where *had* I seen this before: the same deft flick of the wrist, the match extinguished as she exhaled . . . The coffee warmed me through, and she refilled my cup before speaking.

'What's your business here?'

'I got sick of the towns. The cities. Kept moving west. Every time I settled, two months later, some of them land-claim folks would move in. Not my kind of folks. Home-steaders. Barn dances and hoedowns and preachin' and some plaid-shirted son of a gun figuring a woman on her own only needs his company to make her life complete. I moved. Then I heard there was a place a woman could hang her hat up without any trash bothering her. So I came here.'

Suzanna nodded slowly.

'So what's your business?'

'I write. Used to work back East on a newspaper, only I dug up a little too much high-society scandal. Things got – hot. I did Chicago for a while. Same thing. That time they burned down the newspaper office. I got me a bad name. Got paid not to work in Louisiana.'

'So who're you snoopin' for here?'

It was a damn good thing I didn't have to lie to Suzanna. I couldn't have done it. Her intense blue eyes were still and blazing. Instead, I laughed.

'I've retired, Suzanna. I've done my snooping for the right side of the law. I done it – but so good, I found the best of the right side is worse than the worst of the wrong side. And they got money and privilege to prove it. I figured to settle down and write the story of my life.'

Suzanna exhaled smoke in a ripple of perfect rings.

'Seems to me we could use you round here,' she said. Again I had that flash of recognition. But my memory came up with nothing.

'One of these days I'll tell you the story of my life. Yeah. I'll tell you my philosophy, too.' She leaned forward and transfixed me with those eyes of smouldering blue. 'You give any motherfucker one chance and they'll put you six foot under.'

She sat back again.

'Yeah,' she said, flinging one long leg across the other, 'that's what it comes down to. I've seen it. Hell, you could put my life in one of them yellow-back novels, and people wouldn't believe it.'

She rose and stretched like a fine-bred horse.

'I got things to do,' she said. 'Make yourself at home. Get a bath. It'll be good to have some conversation round here again. Grits'll fix us a meal as soon as. Grievous'll sort you out some fresh duds. Be seein' you.'

She made her exit.

17

FIVE

I found my way to the bathroom, where Grievous was growling some tune or other to death.

'Suzanna?' she called as she heard my footsteps.

'No.'

'Come on in. Don't be proud.'

Grievous was lying in a tub of foam in the steamy room.

'Takin' advantage,' she said. 'How d' it go, Typewriter?'

'OK,' I said, shrugging. 'Seems to think I'll be OK to stay.'

'That is a relief to me,' said Grievous. 'Ain't been no new faces round here since Angel, and that's been a pretty passel of horseshit. Suzanna's been twitchy. But she'll tell yuh what yuh need to know. I won't be long here.'

'Suzanna said you'd find me some fresh duds.'

'Waaall, *ainchuh* privileged!' said Grievous. 'Hop in here and I'll do that thing.'

I lay back in the hot suds. I could have slept like a baby. Then I saw a picture on the wall, through the steam. I sat up and stared. A two-foot poster behind glass. It was Suzanna, all right, either that or her twin, only she was dolled up like a fancy woman, all red petticoats and black lace.

And then it all came back to me.

Crazy Man's Coolee. Twenty years or more past.

Coolee was a ramshackle hell-raising town got the Crazy Man tag added when a Bible-thumping wagonload made the mistake of losing their way and stopping there one Sunday. Bent Ashley, the owner of the one big saloon in the place, had lurched into the street to welcome them. There always was a welcome for strangers in Coolee. And it being the Sabbath, Ashley was done up to the eyeballs in his Sunday best: a purple silk number slashed to one muscular thigh, a Spanish black lace fan, rhinestone ear-rings and a choker to match.

'Come and have a drink on the house, folks!'

But Bent Ashley was six foot tall and wore a huge red beard as well as the dress, and the Bible-thumpers rode out of town in an axle-breaking cloud of dust. They spread rumours about Coolee, and, then on, bands of folks would come to stare like we were a freak show. I had come to Coolee after the mayor and chief constable of New York had advised me to go lose myself or get wasted. With the hush money they'd given me at gunpoint I figured to retire some place folks would ask no questions and leave a woman alone to live her life. Bent Ashley's was the only bar I've ever hit outside of a city where the women can look at the women and the men can look at the men and no one gives a goddam. I was happy there for a few years; the town was booming and the land was good.

But the Bible-thumpers' rumours spelt death to the place. All sorts of petty criminals fetched up there with the idea that *their* kind of anything goes; we had an annual invasion of God's ministers besides, come to preach us the evil of our ways, and the longest any of them stayed was three weeks.

The town was getting to be full of lowlife scum and brawling. And then we had a killing – Kate Comstock, a woman who liked her own company, found dead and mutilated. She was a woman kept herself quiet, like I did, maybe sharing a drink on a Saturday night. We had our suspicions about who did it, only no way of proving it and marshals crawling all over the place. I was getting itchy to move on. Again. That remote little spread of mine began to feel dangerous where it had started out feeling like home.

It was one evening after the murder that I'd seen Suzanna, billed as 'The Queen of the Dance' in Bent Ashley's. Odds were high against her being a woman, but when she sashayed down the curved stairs to the stage, there was no doubt in anyone's mind. Competition for the boys! We had us some rednecks in town, whooping and boozing, annoying the women and insulting the men. Bent Ashley was keeping an eye on them: rumour was it was them who'd done the murder. And the rest. Bent Ashley was working up to banning them or worse. It was a bad-feeling night.

But Suzanna had a voice like diamonds and velvet and crooned a tune so sweet the noise died down. I was feeling kinda disgusted at how she made up to the rednecks, twitching a boa over their heads and them crowing – like, *they's one gal in this pansy town tuh appreciate a red-blood male!* – didn't they just love it? In the second half, she drew one of them on stage with her, strutting his lousy gristle like a fool. And then she asked for a drumroll . . . struck a match on her shoe, placed a cheroot in his grinning lips, and drew a gun. The fool was so full of himself, he didn't know what was happening. Something was wrong.

'Stand real still, mister,' cooed Suzanna. 'Ladies and gentlemen, I am about to shoot this cee-gar from this brave man's lips!'

But the shot went straight through his brains, and she turned on the redneck table and hollered, *'This is for my sister, you bastards!'*

Gunsmoke filled the room, shots roared through the smoke, and in the mayhem, I saw her scarlet-clad figure eel up the stairs. The good ole boys were dead. All six of them. She carried a neat trigger.

I dived out the back to see a shadowy figure leap on a horse, tearing a sequinned comb from her hair. Suzanna. She stopped when she saw me.

'What're you going to do about it?' she snarled, drawing her gun.

'Don't worry about a thing,' I said. 'Ride on!'

'I'm riding,' she said. 'I could use your silence.'

'You got it,' I said.

And she was gone. I stuck around just long enough in

Crazy Man's Coolee to dig up everything needed to prove the redneck guilt, and have the case closed. We all played dumb about the avenging angel who'd ridden into town that morning, done what she came for in the evening and vanished before midnight. Me and Bent Ashley rode out of Coolee together, once that was done. He was going back East, he said he could find a dive to hide in, in the city. And I started out due west, always a little ahead of what they like to call civilization.

I towelled myself dry and wiped the steam from the picture: it was her all right. *Suzanna, the Queen of the Dance.* Goddam! It would be one helluva life to write about! She couldn't have been more than seventeen in Crazy Man's Coolee. And what had she done for an encore in the twenty years or so since?

SIX

'This place is a goddam fortress – naturally!' said Suzanna, pouring bourbon after the best meal I'd eaten in years. 'They used to call it Kimama, when the Indians were here. On account of there's butterflies thick as treacle on every tree for about three weeks in the year. Even now the butterflies come, and the Indians have been wiped out as good as. When I came here, it was called Fortress, for reasons your aching bones know too well. I been here some time, and still we don't got a name sits easy, do we, Grievous?'

'I like the butterfly one,' said Grievous surprisingly. 'Only there's been a lot of stuff gone down here ain't too pretty.'

'Well, Typewriter, maybe you'll find us a name.'

'She done my name,' said Grievous. 'She done good there.'

I figured that was the best move I'd made since I'd

21

started through the pass. It was clear Grievous held a lot of sway around Suzanna, and she was the kind you want with you, not against. She tore at the loaf on the table like the crust was rice paper. There was an animal strength in her that I trusted.

'So now you're rested and fed,' said Suzanna, a gold toothpick in her fingers, 'suppose you tell us what you heard on the other side of the pass.'

I told her about the wild wimmin and cayn-ee-bals: she laughed and her eyes demanded more.

'Well,' I said, 'it's kinda confusing. The old guy said something about a woman called Lorraine having a spread out here.'

I watched her face: had she, as I suspected, ousted or wiped out Lorraine? But her faraway eyes showed nothing.

'That's my other name. LaReine. Suzanna LaReine. It's French: means the queen.'

'Like that picture you got upstairs?' I said.

'I was my daddy's little princess,' she cut in smoothly. 'And I'll tell you about that picture some other time.'

The subject was closed.

'Well, Grievous,' said Suzanna, when we'd lowered the golden line in the bourbon bottle a good two inches, 'you better get back to the bunkhouse and see what gives. Tomorrow I want you all up here for an early start. I got a few things I need to tell you about.'

'Sure,' said Grievous, rising. 'She – ?'

'She's staying up here. For the moment.'

Suzanna put two fingers on my wrist, and looked at Grievous. My flesh burned where she touched me, and I fought a blush.

'Well, sure, Suzanna.' Grievous was clearly not happy.

'What is it?' snapped Suzanna with a touch of impatience.

'It's goddam Angel is what it is!' roared Grievous. 'Yer

business is yer own, Suzanna, but that one is getting me real nervous.'

'Well now,' said Suzanna, her face darkening. 'Is that so? You tell our hot-headed little Angel I'll talk to her tomorrow.'

'Well, OK,' said Grievous. 'But I'm warnin' yuh, Suzanna, you'll need more than words fer that one.'

She slapped her hat against her knee and left, muttering good night to the old lady who'd eaten out on the porch, still sulking, Suzanna said, over having the hog's piss she called coffee called hog's piss.

'Besides, Fingerbone can't handle living in a house,' she added. 'I fixed her up a room and a bed and found her rolled up in a blanket on the goddam floor. She's too old to change.'

Suzanna rose, picked up the bourbon and nodded to me to follow her. She went into a wood-panelled room with a huge desk and safe as well as deep armchairs, where we sat.

'My office,' she said, pouring drinks. Then she looked at me. It was a sombre appraising look. 'Seems to me – aw, I dunno,' she said. 'Are you figuring on staying around?'

'Are you asking? If you are – '

'I never ask anyone to stick around without reasons. And I always let 'em know my reasons. There's going to be changes round here. And soon. Lotsa paperwork, lotsa talking. I could use you there. I kinda like the idea of you writing the story of my life. Might make things a sight clearer to all those folk wearin' my name out. And I could use someone to talk to. Fingerbone's drank away what brain she ever had, which wasn't a lot to start with; Grievous got the best muscle I ever met. Only she don't think things through. And the rest are fine – for shootin' and ropin' and stuff. One thing we all got here is I'm the boss. My spread, my decisions, my ass in Alcatraz if it comes to it.'

23

She paused and lit a pencil-thin cheroot.

'I like you, too. I got a feel for people. Are you staying, Typewriter?'

It was a challenge.

I thought a while. Bosses I never have been able to stick and the feeling has gone both ways. I don't take orders from anyone. But Suzanna had been talking to me as an equal. Years before when she'd said she could *use* my silence, I'd gone my own way as always and spoken out in print to keep the heat off her trail. I looked her in the eye. There was a story here like no one had ever dreamed of. Maybe the best story I'd ever write. And there was also Suzanna . . .

'Yeah,' I said, raising my glass. 'I'm staying.'

SEVEN

When I rose next morning, the sun was blazing through the blind. I made my way downstairs to a murmur of voices that ceased as I appeared. Suzanna was pacing the floor, her crew around her, some standing, some sitting, Grievous shifting from one heavy-booted foot to another.

'Good morning,' said Suzanna, her eyes on me. 'Sleep OK?'

Every other eye in the room was on her, except Angel's: that dangerous cerulean blaze flickered between me and Suzanna, and she set her mouth in an ugly line.

'Some of you met my friend here yesterday. She'll be living in the house from now on. Time we had some education round here. Could be useful.'

'For what?' snarled Angel.

'For keepir ʒ dumb asses like yours outta jail for a start, Angel. Besides, me and Typewriter go back a long way.'

'Yeah?' jeered Angel.

'Shaddap, Angel,' growled Grievous as a scarlet flush

rose on Suzanna's neck. I expected her to strike Angel, bring her to heel somehow; one look at Mercedes's vicious face and the frank disbelief on everyone else's confirmed this. No one challenges a woman like Suzanna and gets away with it. So why did she let the colour die in her face before speaking? She said only:

'Angel, you and me have talking to do. Later. This evening.'

'Maybe I'm busy,' said Angel, like a petulant child.

'And maybe you'll just get your butt up here when I tell you.'

An uneasy silence, broken by Grievous's shuffling toe-caps, and a sudden cackle from the door: Fingerbone waving her battered flask.

'Whup the bitch, Suzanna! Goddam, yuh've had better than that cleanin' yuh boots with they tongue! Tell her!'

'Jesus, Fingerbone, I'll do things my way.'

'Yer gettin' soft!' The old woman glared. 'This whelp here ain't house-trained yit, only been busted out fer two months, and she's acting like *she's* the goddam queen! Go on, hit me, Suzanna, hit an old lady. My hide don't feel nothin' anyways. *I'm makin' coffee.*'

The kitchen door slammed. A volley of curses shattered through the wood: Grits didn't want no one friggin' around with her ******* wood range, particularly some ***** ********* ****** old ******* like Fingerbone.

Lucille tipped her hat over her brow. 'Kin I say something here, Suzanna?'

Suzanna waved her arm, and leaned back against the wall.

Lucille stood up. 'Just got one thing to say, girls. Most of us had the best times of our life here. Speakin' personally, I'm pig-sick with all this goddam bitchin' and arguin' like we never had before. Last few months been hell. Ever since you, Assassina, and you, Angel, got here.'

'Yer damn right, Lariat,' said Roo. 'I figure the both of yuh shape up or ship out. This the only damn place

25

women like us can have any kind of life. And I don't figure to break up my happy home for the pair of yuh.'

'Don't put me alongside of her!' flashed Assassina, springing to her feet.

'I put yuh together. Grow up and I'll start seein' yuh separate.'

'OK,' said Suzanna. 'I've been making allowances for you both, seein' as you was just sprung. You're right, Lucille, Roo, Grievous. If either one of you plans on stayin', jest calm down. We got enough to fight outside without fighting between ourselves. Assassina, Angel – are you with us? Or are you leaving?'

The last was drawled, like who-gives-a-damn-and-it-sure-ain't-me.

Assassina was the first to shrug and say it was OK with her.

'OK with me too, Mercedes,' said Suzanna. 'Angel?'

Angel glared at her. 'You know it's OK with me. Where else do I have to go?'

'We'll talk later,' said Suzanna.

I was riveted. Suzanna's cool could have snuffed out a volcano quicker than blink, and here she was pussyfooting around an overgrown fire-eater. There was something behind this kid-glove approach I couldn't work out.

'Now,' said Suzanna, 'we got business to do. You all must have been aware of a certain flash-britches rancher rode in here three weeks back. Mr Darknell van Doon. He's got the idea he wants to make some kinda partnership in the valley. He calls it Fortress. As you know, I've never been crazy about that name. Talking to Grievous last night, we reckon it's time to go back to calling the place Kimama.'

'What's that?' said Mercedes.

'Butterfly. The Indians used to call it that.'

'I don't get it,' said Mira languidly. 'I'm here because I don't like no men, Suzanna, don't want shit to do with 'em. Who is this Darknell van Doon?'

'Don't worry none,' said Suzanna. *'Grits! Fingerbone!* Get your ornery asses in here pronto – this is to do with you too.'

Grits and Fingerbone jostled through the kitchen doorway, cursing royally.

'Siddown and quit belly-aching,' said Suzanna. 'I never aimed on setting up in partnership with no man, and I ain't about to change my ways now. Besides, I got partners: the lot of you, my family. But I had this kinda sense I'd better hear out this Mr Darknell van Doon: he wasn't a man just talking for himself, y' unnerstand. He was talking for a firm. A big organization that would git federal over his disappearance. He came along with a proposal. I've been chewing it over ever since, and I'm gonna put it to you all. Then we can decide.'

EIGHT

'Mr Darknell van Doon,' said Suzanna, blowing smoke, 'has access to numerous cattle accounts. We're not talking regular ranchers, we're talking eastern folks and folks from England who don't know the ass of a steer from its hooves. But they're kinda free with paper money, and into what they call investment. They want to pay out money and have folk buy and raise and tend and graze their cattle, and never see hide nor hair of any of them. They want figures setting pretty on paper and gitting bigger every year. Percentages and profits. And Mr Darknell van Doon seems to think this here valley, *Fortress*, holds some of the best grazing land this far west. Which is true. I got the idea he'd do anything to move in, and had the bucks to back him. And when I say he'd do *anything* I ain't talking bushwhackers, ain't talking regular cowboys who kin take a warning like we can dish out. I'm talking if there's one shot rings out and hits the yaller flesh of his hirelings, the place'll be crawling with feds. You can appreciate why I had to burn so much of my damn time talking to the motherfucker.'

'Suzanna,' said Lariat Lucille, 'I coulda sworn yuh never wanted cattle tramplin' this land. With you it's grullas . . . me too. Yuh tellin' me we gotta have a bunch of cowboys ropin' steers here? It'd be like havin' the in-laws campin' on the porch. Kinda provokin'.'

'Sheee-it!' exploded Suzanna. 'Don't I know it? Anyways, I figured out a scheme. Mr Darknell van Doon is planning to drag his linen-tight ass back this way in two weeks. That's all the time we've got to get ourselves organized.'

'Whaddya mean – organized?' said Mira, scowling.

Suzanna's mouth made a slow grim smile. 'You'd a been proud of me!' she said. 'Specially you, Typewriter! Hell, you should a heard the story I cooked up for him! Whiles you all was frettin' about with yer damned ears rubbin' the shine offa the keyholes, I was havin' me some fun. I've always been a hell of a good liar, particularly when talkin' to fools. Here's van Doon, sittin' his ass on my furniture, feet on my floor, guzzlin' my liquor and smokin' my cheroots. He wuz doin' all a hawg knows how to be charmin' to a lady, which he weren't and I ain't.

'"Miz Comstock," says he, "you could make yourself a pile of money outta cattle on this land here."

'I sat forward a little, and shook my head kinda sorrowful.

'"Don't think it hasn't crossed my mind many a time, Mr van Doon," says I, real earnest.

'"Ey – and I am the one to git you tuh realizin' that dream," says he. "Do we got ourselves a partnership agreement?"

'Out comes his hand for me to shake, as if I'd filthy my flesh pressin' his sweatin' palm! As if I was yesterday's little lady fool who'd sign away her life on the say-so of a stranger! Van Doon don't listen to no one without they're tellin' him yes!

'"It cain't be done!" I say, and start pacin' the floor, kinda agitated. "Come over here by the window, Mr van Doon – what do you see out there?"

'"Waaall, hills, Miz Comstock," says he, wonderin' if he's got himself a crazy woman to do business with.

'"Hills!" says I. "Hills? I wisht it was just hills. Them *hills* look real purdy, don't they? Like a slice of Gawd's own heaven, don't they? But them's the hills I see in nightmares, Mr van Doon. Covered with forests, and riddled with caves, so a man didn't know his way could spend twenty years goin' in circles and never see his wife nor child again. A man could go up on them hills and die – or get murdered."

'"You ain't tellin' me they's Injuns up there?" says van Doon, gettin' all hot and excited, like *this is man's work.* "We kin smoke 'em out, Miz Comstock, they's laws and reservations for their kind now!"

'"Indians?" I says. "Any Indians in them hills given us no pain nor grief. We got no quarrel with 'em. We seems to be able to live side by side without a whole heap of trouble."

'"Ho!" says van Doon, puttin' on his Daddy-knows-best voice. "We'll see! I cain't see our investors takin' too well to devil-worshippin' an' human sacrifice in the vicinity of their hard-earned investments!"'

'He said *what*?' This came in a growl from Lucille.

'Honey, that was only the start of it! More I heard, more I called to mind a trip I took once and come across a real evil slurry of hot mud spewin' outta the ground, stinkin' and writhin' like the guts of a fresh-killed wild dog. What that boy do have swirlin' around in his head brought the bile risin' to my throat! So I stopped his foolishness, set him down again with a fresh glass of liquor.

'"Mr van Doon," I told him, "you listen to me and you listen good. Where you see hills and forests and *imagine* stuff I never come across outside of a picture book, a wicked man sees the best hide-outs in this whole country! Caves God himself couldn't find, paths that twist back on 'emselves afore they get to plungin' over ravines. And *that's* what we got to fear from them hills. Crawlin' like an ant heap with the scummiest stage-robbin', jail-bustin', castle-rustlin' murderous lowlife ever drew breath! If you could clean them out from around here, you could retire and live like a king on the bounty money!"

'"Waaall, do say, Miz Comstock!" says our boy. "We'll get the law in! And th' army!"

'"Law?" I says to him, like the word gives me a pain in the gut, which it does, only not for the reasons I give him. "Law? The law won't touch these boys. See, they hightail outta this valley an' do their murderin' an' robbin', then they hightail it back and cain't nobody locate their rat's nests. You ever heard of Elias Burke, the bounty hunter?"

'"That's the man to do it,' says van Doon, like I knew he would. "Elias Burke's brought in nigh on three hunnerd lawbreakers."

'"We found his body feedin' the crows and plucked near clean not a half-day's ride from here a year ago. And Tracker Parker? Him that brought in the Gordon Gang? Found 'im frozen stiff hangin' from a tree by the pass last Christmas Day. Sign tied around his neck saying BE WARNED, and every letter writ in his own blood."

'Well, van Doon is beginnin' to look a little sick as them rolls and wads of greenbacks he's been dreamin' of start to float further and further away. I could see his mind shiftin' around every which way, then he looks at me real innocent and says, "How come they leave *you* be, Miz Comstock? Kinda gallant way of actin' for trash like that, what with you bein' a woman and a mighty fine looker, too, ma'am."

'I had to shove my hands in my pockets to hold back from crackin' his head, only I found I din' have no pockets, bein' as I'd got myself rigged up in that damn dress a yours, Fingerbone. It's a rusty ole black one, Typewriter, but seemed the most fittin' garment around here for a widder lady gittin' called on by a gentleman. Hah! So I look down in some confusion and look up real slow. And I give him the scam.

'"Mr van Doon," I say, "you see these widow's weeds on my back?"

'"Yes, ma'am," says he, rememberin' to look respectful.

'"Well, this is family business, but I guess I'll have to tell you," I say, like it's breakin' my heart. "Years ago, me and Mr Comstock come out here to make our claim, have ourselves a homestead and raise us a family. My husband – my late husband – wasn't an easy man and didn't take to city livin'. He'd quarrelled with his family, quarrelled with his business partners, and we were out to make a fresh start where couldn't nobody bother him. Well, one day he went out on the hills to check his traps, and I'm waitin' for him at home, cookin' as fine a supper as a woman knows how. Only it got late and he didn't come back. I commenced to frettin' like a woman does and finally, round midnight, I picked up his twelve-bore and a storm lantern and set out to find him. I found him."

'"Dead?" says van Doon.

'"If I hadn't knowed every patch and darn in his shirt and pants, I wouldn't a knowed it was him. Death must a been a blessed release from torment. His body and face was pulp."

'"Waaall, that settles, it," says van Doon. "Only a Injun could act that way."

'"Mr van Doon," I say, "have you ever seen an Indian with a beard striped black and white and bushy like a skunk? With one eye brown, the other milk-blue blind, and a scar like lightnin' from his brow clear across his nose to the other cheek?"

'"There's only one man on this earth looks like that," says he, "and that's No Arms Hackmore . . . you tellin' me *he's* in them thar hills?"

31

'"None other," I say.

'Now, No Arms Hackmore really set our boy to wonderin'. Seein' as No Arms acquired his name from the signature he left on all his victims, seein's how he's the most feared lawbreaker of 'em all, totin' a damn sabre and a belt bristlin' with knives, and how he has a gang riding with him each one worse than the next, finally van Doon is listenin' to me.

'"Yes," I said, real soft. "When I come round from faintin', that's the face I see lookin' down on me, as I lay beside the mutilated corpse of Mr Comstock. Seems that some of No Arms's boys come across my husband and figure he should share the contents of his traps with 'em. I told you, my husband wasn't slow to pick hisself a fight, and that's just what he done. They treated him the way they'd a treated anyone gave 'em no. But No Arms warn't too pleased. Said they was no need to have killed him, and seein' as that made me a helpless woman all alone in the world, somethin' made him take pity on me. He swore to leave me and mine in peace, and I haven't seen him from that day to this. But what he says goes for every gang up there."

'"And you figger," said van Doon, "you figger that bringin' a cattle ranch to this here valley of Fortress'd stir up the whole stinkin' nest of 'em?"

'"There ain't no question," I said to him. "Think about it any way you choose, Mr van Doon, it ain't gonna happen."'

'So how d'you leave it?' said Grievous.

'Waaall, he's gone back west to work out some sort of plan. He's got the impression that most a this valley's my land which it ain't, only I live here like we all do. He left still puffin' an' blowin' about th' army. I told him No Arms would have seen him now and know his face. He didn't like that a whole heap. He ain't entirely sure yet that we're all women. He is one determined pile of greed, that boy! So we should back up all that No Arms Hackmore bull for

32

when he comes back. Burn out the land west a here, make it look like the *outlaws* ain't too pleased. Which we ain't. Whaddya think?'

'I don't like it, Suzanna,' said Grievous heavily. 'Short term, fine. But we all know this place – Kimama – it's heaven on earth. You put a dyin' steer on the grass here and it'll be frisky as a dogie in twenty-four hours. Why, that deadbeat mare Typewriter come in on – she's born again in less than a day. Any cattle we git here gonna grow so fat and luscious, folk gonna be askin' questions. And questions mean civilized folks comin' fer a look-see, and then there's marshals, and every kind of trouble brewin'.'

'Surely t' hell we kin shoot 'em out?' said Roo. 'Done it before, Suzanna.'

'You ask Typewriter here,' said Suzanna. 'The world is changing faster than a snowball melts in the sunshine. Tell 'em Typewriter. What happens in the world of big bucks and important men?'

I shifted a little and built myself a smoke. 'The way I know it, these days, bucks talk louder than voices. I tried to keep ahead of it, God knows, coming here, but it seems like you're being squeezed from the east and the west. If this Darknell van Doon is set on pressing a claim, there isn't a way out but compromise. I hate compromise as much as any woman I ever met . . . but the globe is only so big, and this country seems to be getting smaller every day I breathe. You've already got a guard on the eastern pass. As I know. But there is a lot of folk shifted round Kimama and hit the West Coast. The land there is mighty dry, quakes and God only knows what else. Them folks want a slice of the good life. They're greedy. Like Suzanna says, best to fake it we got ourselves a plague of marauding murderers and desperadoes, and hope to put them off that way. And then think what to do next so we can live out our natural here.'

'Suzanna,' said Lariat Lucille, 'yuh don't got to ask

would I follow yuh to the ends of the earth. Wouldn't we be best to light out and find us some other piece of land?'

'For what? Five years? And some other entreprenoor come gunning for us? We hafta make a stand,' said Suzanna, her eyes darkening like the deep blue sea.

'How come we've kept the east away?' demanded Grits shrilly. 'How the hell we done *that* east and cain't do the same west? Make this Death Valley, where folks are skeered to skeeters to stick they noses less'n they git fried?'

'Like I said,' drawled Suzanna, wearily, 'this Mr Darknell van Doon ain't one lonesome cowboy to git picked offa his cayuse to feed the crows. This here is a syndicate. One guy gits rubbed, they's ten worse to fill his two-tone brogues.'

Mary Maloof Fingerbone stood up like one of the furies and shook her wrinkled finger at the group. 'Suzanna! Listen to me! I know yuh think yurr the smartest thing ever straddled a bronc, and yuh got the opinion I'm past anything beyond settin' rockin', but I got thangs tuh tell yuh.'

Suzanna looked pained. She set her jaw. 'Quit your braggin', Fingerbone,' she ordered. 'I know your heart is in the right place and every plaguey day the damn thing starts beatin' again. But we gotta talk business. Jest hush.'

The old woman subsided, muttering, and sucking at the tin neck of her flask. This was more than boozing bragging. Just what did she know? I aimed to find out.

'So I hate this job,' said Suzanna with fire in her voice. 'But this is how it is, unless you got a better idea. Lucille and Roo, best keep an eye out for the east. Grievous and Mercedes, light out for the west and blaze away at the pasture. There's kerosene in the store. And the same every other day for two weeks. And Mira, Angel and me – we'll shift the horses to the east: the scent of smoke's gonna panic 'em to stampeding otherwise.'

'And what's yuh fancy eastern friend gonna do?' demanded Angel, shooting a glance of venom at me.

'My friend here's gonna look through the books,' said Suzanna. 'And if one of you two misbegotten lollygaggers can quit arguin', maybe we can git some coffee round here and get going.'

Grits fixed the ancient Fingerbone with a glare, and stomped back to her kitchen.

'Long shot, Suzanna,' drawled Lucille nonchalantly.

'I never been happy with nothin' else,' said Suzanna.

NINE

Suzanna beckoned me to the study.

'Some files here I'd like you to look through, Typewriter,' she said, indicating a pile of worn manila folders. 'When we're gone.'

I saw them off, marvelling at the sheer drive of the woman who'd brought this hell-raising band together so smoothly and then split them: the fire of Assassina might be fed a little, burning pasture, and Angel was right where Suzanna could keep an eye on her. Something bound the two of them: at first I had thought it was just a tired tale of jaded passion, and who could blame Suzanna for moving in on those good looks? Or Angel for coming right on back? But there had to be something more.

Mary Maloof Fingerbone was staring at me when I turned.

'Suzanna says yer stayin'. And what she says goes with me. But she says yer gonna write the story of her life, and I know that woman fer one braggin' loudmouth always makes herself come out good. So I wanna get a few things straight afore yuh git tuh clackin' out what she chooses to feed yuh. Lemme git another a these. We'll set us a while, you an' me, Typewriter, and there's one chapter in yuh damn book gonna be the truth.'

'Another a these' proved to be a refill of Fingerbone's battlescarred flask, and a glass for me if I cared to wipe out a few billion brain cells. The first sip told me as much, and I added water.

'See here,' she started, lighting one of her polecat maccoboys, 'I'm a woman as knows one end from th' other. Goddammit, when I'm your age, I'm riding alongside a Calamity Jane, and don't you believe none uh that Wild Bill horseshit they spin yah! In love with that soft-bellied showman! In love! Calamity Jane! Call me Carry-Tar-Nation first! I'll see the sun go down in the east afore I take heed a such nonsense! On'y Janey's gittin' old when I fetch up with her. The day she dies, she dies in my arms and the proof of it is I'm theer jest like I'm settin' here right now! She looks up at me and she says, "Mary Maloof, air we goin' west today?" I says, "Sure we're goin' west, Janey, jest as soon as yuh rest yuhself.' Then she closes her eyes like a sleepin' child, and never draws another breath. Yuh credit whut I'm tellin' yuh, Typewriter?'

'Sure,' I said, raising my glass to her colourful memories.

'O . . . K,' said the old lady, sinking a gutful of liquor. 'Waaall – after Janey dies, I'm left at a loose end. Cain't seem to settle no place. Wild Bill finds me a spot in th' show, shooting blanks at greasepaint Injuns, and I travel round that way awhiles. Then one day we find ourselves in Deadwood agin. I have some business there. Whut it is I only got one person to tell to, and it ain't you. There's some trick ridin' goin' on with a rodeo, and we're settin' up fer the next day. I take off tuh the rodeo ring and see a few bucks do their stuff. Next thing I know, I see the sweetest ass I ever did see, in a pair of britches tight like skin, and this ass is about tuh hit the ground! Bronco bustin'! Three minutes and fifty-nine seconds! What a body has tuh do tuh earn her crust! Then this ass gits tuh its feet, and it's a woman. And her mouth throws out a lasso of cussin' like I only ever hear from Janey. Fit to blow the spurs offa all the cowboy crowd there. I says, "Hey, honey, can I give y' a hand?" I git a mouthful bluer than th' Atlantic. Y' unnerstan', she thinks I'm jest another cowpoke. I have short hair at the time. Makes life easier. But I'm tellin' yuh, Typewriter: that moment, I am In Love. But bad. And that sin-blue mouth and sweet ass belong to Suzanna.'

Mary Maloof Fingerbone applied her wrinkled lips to the flask. I sipped so she wouldn't feel isolated.

'Yuh think a mouthful a cussin' might put me off? Honey, it's music tuh my ears. I never hear cussin' so sweet since Janey dies. Suzanna cusses blue like lightnin' at sea, and I'm off thru' the crowd, tuh git tuh the back of the stands afore she puts up and goes. Like I figure, Suzanna LaReine rides alone and likes it that way. But I throw my cards down with Wild Bill that day, and pick me a horse full a lightnin' and take off after her. We camp in the desert and never do the stars look sweeter than that long night by that bitty fire! Suzanna sits there, sharpening her ole bowie knife on the hot stones and tellin' me she don' need *no one* in this life. "*Need*, sugar?" I said. "Comes down tuh it, no woman needs more than a place tuh sleep an' food in her belly. But company comes in useful sometimes. And I been ridin' alone a long whiles. Think of me as yuh bodyguard."

'Yuh look at me now, Typewriter, I ain't shit beyond skin and bones and liquor. But I am the woman who rides side by side with Calamity Jane, Champion Swearer of the Plains: I'm the one they call Poker Annie and a whole lot besides, and I'm the one that sleeps at the door of Suzanna LaReine this eighteen years, and guards her precious life beyond my own! Yiiii-iiizz! When they come to throw these old bones in a trench without no marker, there are papers to help her beyond my grave. Yuh know whut I think?'

I shrugged. Easy-like. I wanted her to go on. She did.

'I believe, and I mean it like gospel, I do believe Sweet Sue – and she'd shoot my tits off fer callin' her that – I know in my bones, and the last few years I know my bones closer 'n a heartbeat, Sweet Sue is the soul reincarnate of Calamity Jane. And I'm the luckiest soul alive tuh ride with th' one, and meet her again when the world is gittin' lonesome fer me. Trouble is Suzanna's born too late, and I fear for her. Times are gone when swaggerin' britches and a tongue like a silver dagger kin dig yuh outta trouble. Those are good days. But this valley'll be good fer as long as I kin keep it that way.'

The old woman's dusty skin was flushed, and she drew again on her flask. Made a disgusted mouth when it was empty. I sipped again at the diluted firewater. Damn! She must have had guts like a horsepower locomotive.

'I jist want yuh t' know,' she hissed, suddenly bleary, 'I jist want yuh tuh git the record straight. I ain't jest some old soak Suzanna takes pity on. Woman's got a heart of pure gold. Lookit whut she does fer Mercedes and goddam Angel! But me, Mary Maloof Fingerbone, I sign on with her the minute I see her! She don't admit it, but I save her butt one or two times . . . and now I ain't even good enough tuh make her coffee! When I'm dead she'll know . . . ask Deadwood!'

And the old woman was asleep. I straightened the blanket over her, extinguished her fetid cigar and placed the drained flask at her side. Time to inspect the files Suzanna had left for me. I went indoors.

TEN

I sat in the oak swivel chair at Suzanna's desk and opened the top file. Years had yellowed the newspaper cuttings pasted on each page, dated in faded ink. The first was some forty years previous, and recorded the birth of twins in Evening Shade: Suzanna Prudence Charity and Sarah Grace Modeste LaReine, sisters to Kate Comstock LaReine, daughters to Gaston Henri LaReine and Eugenia Comstock LaReine.

The next entry was ten years later: one small paragraph about a mysterious fire that had gutted the LaReine place, leaving the twins and their sister Kate orphans. All three were thrown on the mercy of the Temperance Chapel of Righteousness, there being no estate. At the head of the next page was a lettered heading: WHO TOOK US IN, and a list of names and dates. The list then split into two columns, one headed ME, the other, SARAH, MY SISTER. And not a word about big sister Kate.

The twin orphans had spent no more than three months with any one of these families. The one before they'd been split up had lasted only a week. There were intricate marks by all the names, crosses and circles, and the letters d and a, like a code. The household where they'd been for a week was scored underneath three times.

And just what had they done to be moved so often? What had been done to them? When they were parted, Suzanna went to the Reverend Obadiah Hough in Helena, Arkansas, and Sarah to the Reverend John Lippincott in Ada, Oklahoma. Rough travelling between in those days – the twins would probably have never seen each other. They didn't last long in these holy households, either. Still they shifted – Kansas, Colorado, Missouri – and always with a reverend's family.

I turned the page. Another news clipping, announcing the death of Sarah Grace Modeste LaReine, after a fever. And an old envelope, creased a hundred times and smoothed out. Inside it a ragged piece of paper:

Dear Sis,
I get no better here as the days go by. The air here is like breathing steam, and I can keep nothing down. I have the feeling I'm not long for this world, and would like nothing better than

to see your face before I go. But the Rev says this is impossible, and we must just pray. Best I can do is sneak a look in the glass. I guess you are still the same as me to look at, only I hope a lot healthier than the pale face I see. Sis, I learned you can be sixteen in a lot of places and get away from your 'family' and no law to bring you back. So best of luck. If I was going to live, I'm sure of one thing, I'd leave here and we'd meet again and find Kate and be a family again. We've been too long among strangers.

They're back from the meeting-house, I must go. God knows when you'll get this, Suzanna, think of me as I do you, always.

Sarah.

From the date, the twins were then fifteen and a half. Sarah had died barely a week after she'd written this sad little letter.

Suzanna had lit out of her Missouri home the same year – there was a crude handbill pasted in of Singing Suzanna, the Gal with the Golden Guitar. This was back in the town of her birth, Evening Shade. A plethora of handbills charted a strange zigzag journey, and here and there was the name Kate and a question mark. From Evening Shade to Glory; Burning Gulch to Damnation; Sweet Springs, Markhanita, Avarice, Thunder Falls . . . Suzanna had sung and searched right across the states for her sister, her last living relative.

The handbills became more professional, the Gal with the Golden Guitar became Suzanna, the Queen of Song, or Suzanna, Queen of the Dance, like the full-colour picture in the bathroom upstairs. She wasn't more than seventeen at the point she hit Crazy Man's Coolee . . .

She'd made a double page spread for that.

KATE COMSTOCK LAREINE was lettered at the top left-hand side, with her birth date. Then a list – Suzanna liked lists – of every town Kate'd lived in, and what she'd done there: mostly farming, and riding for various outfits. Finishing up with Crazy Man's Coolee, and the newspaper account of her horrific murder and how there were no suspects yet: '*Miss Comstock lived very quietly and had no enemies.'* But she was a woman living on her own – a target for scorn and contempt. I recalled the snarling pack of human coyotes who'd done for her. Over the page was a list of their names in furious red, bracketed together. By the bracket was a word in black blocks: GUILTY, and a flourishing signature: *Suzanna LaReine*. And the date. The day I'd first seen her; the day she'd wiped from the face of the earth the red-blooded *real men* who'd brutally destroyed the last bit of family she'd travelled so hard and far to find.

And then she had written across the foot of the page: KATE COMSTOCK LAREINE: MURDERED, AVENGED AND NEVER FORGOTTEN. This grim documentation was followed by a blank page. But then I started with recognition: here were my own newspaper articles following Suzanna's disappearance. We'd run a special edition of the paper once the evidence had been pieced together, with lurid sketches of the murderers and a daguerreotype likeness of Kate Comstock at the top of every page. She'd dropped the LaReine – I wondered why. Too easy to trace? Suzanna'd know. That edition of the paper was trial by print. I spoke of an unknown woman driven to take matters into her own hands where the law had failed. There was a whole lyrical summing-up of the case – the murdering scum would have hanged anyway, and, I'd argued, what right had anyone to bring to justice a woman who had shown us all the meaning of Justice where the Law had failed? Finally I had appealed to the sensitive pockets of the good citizens to decide if they wanted good money spent pursuing this unknown avenger, when there was surely crime enough to occupy more sheriffs and marshals than we could afford.

I grinned ruefully as I read it all through. I was some crusader in those days, and my fingers had burned along the typewriter keys, unleashing all my righteousness and my anger at having let my silence be bought in New York. But what else do you do with the barrel of a Colt at your head, and a deep undraggable river the only other prospect being offered? You take the money and go. I'd told myself this a thousand times since, but it didn't make me feel any better.

I guessed Suzanna must have worked out who I was the day before when I had outlined why I wanted to stay here in Kimama. Leaving this file was her way of letting me know that. That was what she meant by she liked me and we went back a long way. I decided to build a smoke, drink some coffee and take some fresh air before I delved through the rest of the folder.

ELEVEN

Old Lady Fingerbone was snoring as I sauntered out into the dazzling day. I took the leaf-shaded path up behind the house, which would give me a view of the valley. Grass brushed my knees on this little-used track, and a light scent of clover rose around me. The tree trunks were silver, birch split and whorled with growth, mountain ash dusted with russet and ochre lichen stars. Great groves of sighing cottonwood gave way to swathes of evergreen, and the grass thinned out to lusty curls of fern. There is always a waiting silence in pine woods and the scent of spruce and cedar urged me upwards.

The path looped down a grassy ridge, thigh-deep silver-green sea lavish with flowers, nodding and drowsy with bees and butterflies like flying jewels. The liquid song of a mountain stream came through the wild meadow. Soon the dusty path spread into sandy fingers, flattened out like a pressed tree root along the curvaceous banks. The water was quick and shallow, and here and there had eaten away a great shelf of bank and built itself a golden pool where fallen blossom skated against the dancing dazzle of the sun. The path picked up on the opposite bank, sweeping from a small sandy shore to disappear among the waving grass. I sat a while and let smoke make blue eddies along the water. I rolled off my boots to wade across, but stopped halfway when a tantalizing view came into sight upstream. The banks twisted so sharply that this had been hidden from where I'd been sitting.

Blue shadows of distant trees masked a silver cascade thin as a ribbon: I felt irresistibly drawn there, and waded along, the soft silt and smooth pebbles of the streambed cooling my feet. I might have been the first person ever in this luxuriant jungle, grasses and reeds towering above my head. Each new turn in the stream's course brought the alluring silvery ribbon a little closer, and the sound of rushing water grew louder as I walked. Now I had to duck branches outflung at shoulder level, and lower: I was practically crawling along a tunnel of leaves and trees and water. When I could straighten up again, I was cramped with stooping and suddenly blinded by the magnificent abundance of a waterfall cascading into a silver-sheened pool. I flung my boots to the furthest bank, and plunged in over my head.

The water tugged me around like a floating log, and I closed my eyes against the bright blue sky, drifting. All at once I was ducked and tumbled and shot up gasping under the icy force of the mountain cataract. Oh, yeah! I dived back for more, used all my strength to punch the sheer white torrent and hold my place, wrestling, nose-diving, crashing head over heels through darkness and shooting up like a cork, only to be shoved deeper by the might of the flow.

Finally I was exhausted and made for the shore where my boots had landed. I stripped off my clothes and spread them out on flat rocks to dry.

I must have dozed off, and woke to a deep humming, rustling sound – all around me, welling from the heart of the pool and the towering bluff, drowning even the loud arpeggio of the waterfall, throbbing from the very sky. I could see nothing different, and sat up. A moving million-leaved cloud of colour appeared, hovering over the pool, but as I leaned forward, it disappeared, as I leaned back it came into view again.

There and not there . . . my skin tingled, and my heart beat fast at the fantastic living beauty. Kimama! Butterflies! I had never seen so many clustered together in such a rainbow. Their wings whirred with the sound of spring breezes in an aspen tree; the form of the cloud shifted to a sphere, belled out to a giant egg, then thinned lazily to a spiral and moved up the foamy torrent to vanish as if through a doorway. The humming ceased.

'Kimama!' I said aloud, and heard the echo of my voice behind me.

'Kimama!' Deep and slow, like an oak tree talking.

I turned.

An Indian woman was standing behind me, still as a rock. She was tall, her copper skin lean and muscled. Her eyes met mine and a shiver ran up my spine. For her eyes were brilliant green, shining like a witch-ball at full moon. Time got lost in those eyes, playing every memory of leaves, ferns, fronds, mosses, jewels; the fire colours sparked from the eyes of a night-prowling cat surprised in a beam of light. All this, and more. She was one of the wise women, marked and chosen by those viridian eyes. She looked into my soul and it was a warm look. She knew – me, and everything, it felt like.

She sat beside me, legs crossed. Her cheeks bore intricate twin tattoos of winged snakes – maybe dragons – and the same creatures flowed along and around her arms between broad copper bands.

'Kimama,' she said gravely, and swept one arm around to include the whole place.

I built a smoke and handed her the makings. She took the pouch, and we smoked together.

'Blimey, what wind blew you in here?' she said.

'My life is a pact with chance,' I said, figuring to keep my cards close to my chest.

'That's a good one, duchess,' she said. 'I seen you from the cliff, and seen you chuck them boots. Right on the spot, mate. The sacred spot where the vision is to be seen. You gave me a turn there, all right. I thought I was the only one knew this place. You don't know what I'm on about, eh, duchess?'

I tried to place her accent. There was strength in her voice, deep like the current muscling along a powerful river, and carefree like a dash of sea foam; dancing over this was a chirpiness I'd heard somewhere before.

'No,' I said. 'I saw the butterflies – then I didn't. What does it mean?'

'Now you see them, now you don't, all right. They're on their way. They'll be in the valley in three weeks. My old people had a story about them. They said they sent their spirit ahead to see if the place was suitable, and if it was, they'd come. Oh, there's a lot more with it.'

'Tell me,' I said.

'First they float like a cloud above the world, to see better. If they like what they see, they make the shape of the world. If it still looks good, they make the egg, to show they'll breed again this year. Then the axle-spring to affirm, *they're on their way*. First thing they seen here must have been you, all starkers. They must have been well pleased.'

She ran her eyes over my body and grinned. I returned the compliment.

'Well, we've had a smoke, duchess,' she said. 'You want to smoke the four-rayed herb of seven-petalled joy? It binds those who share it as the vine entwines the tree. For that we need to change names, the old people always said.'

'OK,' I said.

'I have many names,' she said. 'Me Old China is what Charlie called me. He was a good bloke. China is a great

45

country many miles away. Me Old Darling, he called me too. My mother called me Rainbow-Wings by the Rushing Waters. I was born on this spot.'

'Who was Charlie?'

'Be fair, mate!' she said, laughing. 'Else I'll have to call you Parker. It's not much cop to be a Parker, Charlie said. In my language it means one who asks many questions and gives no answers. I'm not proud, sunshine. Maybe your name don't suit you. Give yourself another one. You can do that here.'

I thought of the many names I've taken and been given in my life. The first was a combination of my dead grandmother and my violent father – I'd shed that one the first time I ran away. She'd terrorized my mother while she was alive; after her death, my father had taken over the ceaseless mental and physical brutality, turning her to a screaming shrew. Then he'd figured he could start in on his daughter – me – and I'd lit out. I'd called myself Helena Stanforth, like my mother before the bad day she'd wed. But the city newspapers soon had me down as hard-headed, heartless Helena, the woman who missed her wedding day for a story. I bless that story! Hard-hearted was the politest they'd said. I'd gone back to Helena Stanforth in Coolee to vindicate Suzanna. A dozen names in between, law-abiding and hiding from the law. Now, down at Suzanna's, I was Typewriter. But here, by the falls . . .?

'Call me – hell, I don't know. Give me a name.'

'Blimey, I'm honoured, duchess,' said Me Old Darling, Me Old China, Rainbow-Wings by the Rushing Waters. 'That's what I said to Charlie. It means you're family. We'd better have this smoke first, mate.'

She pulled an old doeskin pouch from her belt, and busied herself with mixing a sweet dried herb into the tobacco. Then handed it to me to light. As I inhaled she said, 'Fools rush in. That's it. Charlie said that to me: Fools rush in where angels fear to tread. You just leaped into the sacred waters, just had a kip on the sacred shore, and just happened to see the vision reserved for the sacred. And here you are, large as life and twice as natural. So that's your name. Fools Rush In.'

Fools Rush In drew deep on the smoke and it filled her body with a sweet dizzy dreaming ecstasy. I handed it to Me Old China.

'Ta, mate,' she said. 'You're a good bloke.'

How do you describe a dream? By the time me and Me Old China had smoked through the four-rayed herb twice, the pool and torrent and trees and rocks and sky were filled with rainbows. And when my eyes met the deep laughing green of hers, she said, 'Well, give us a kiss then. It's a part of the ceremony.'

Just as the earth was alive with brilliant colour, my skin was exquisite cells of light, and when our lips met this rushing fool was an angel with no fear, my feet pure light treading on air, my hands soft-winged, my whole body incandescent sensation.

Another woman's flesh! So strange and new and yet so well known! My fingers traced the muscled smoothness of her back . . . hers mine . . . my lips explored the curve of her cheek and neck . . . hers mine . . . her hands traced and teased my vibrant breasts . . . mine hers . . . our lips and tongues danced a slow waltz . . . my thigh burst into flame between hers between mine . . . head to toe, heads buried in each other's necks, we melted along each other, tongues leaping and pirouetting like fancy dancers on the lava of belly-skin

every quick kiss a flame, every slow touch a forest fire, her thighs now drawing me to the centre of desire that ripples out through every limb, my teeth on her fingertips, her mouth around my hand and so we knew each other's outer skin like our own and so I skate my mouth along the pure sage-sweet sweat of her, plunge head first between her thighs and luxuriate in the wild unknown of that

47

furred cocoon where the bird of paradise waits to be
woken, wild-honey sweetness bursting on my tongue

my whole being welds to hers and there is no separation
as the waters tumble glorious beside us, lips realizing a
starchild speaking ecstasy no words no words and me
to her and she to me, until we are a river in spate,
phosphorescent and mysterious in the land we've found
where we belong because *we know, we know*

We rolled into the deep pool, and jets of steam flung up
forty feet high at the touch of our molten flesh. And then
we cooled to body heat and dripped out onto the shore
with a wonderful lightness, celebrated by the laughter of
the spheres. Back in the world.

Clothes. A smoke. A tobacco smoke.

The sun was going down now, and Me Old China
shrugged like a well-fed tiger.

'I'll be seeing you, Fools Rush In,' she said. 'Now I
know you, strike a light, I do!'

I stood, holding my boots for the tunnel-wade back to
what was now my life.

'You're at Suzanna's gaff, eh?' she said.

'Yes. Since yesterday.'

'You don't hang about, do you, Fools Rush In?' she
said, throwing her head back and laughing like a steer on
loco weed. 'Tell Suzanna I said wotcher. I'll be calling by
soon. Ta-ra!'

She disappeared through the trees.

TWELVE

By the time I got back to the house, thick evening grey
was painted all over the valley. Pasture melted into trees
and the dark sky swallowed the high branches out of
sight. With darkness came a crisp chill and a sprinkle of
glittering stars sharp as diamonds. Lights in the house

made a pale-gold glow from the windows; the house rode the darkness like a galleon at anchor. I stepped on board, to a metallic click of an old Colt ready to spit lead, a vicious red eye glowing and the pungent tang of Mary Maloof Fingerbone's filthy smoke.

'Jest who the hell is that?' The words came out like the skreek of a rusty blade honed on stone.

'Me, Typewriter,' I said.

'Whar the hail yuh bin? We almost sent out a party. Thought yuh'd a bin roped-up over a goddam ant heap by now, waitin' fer a friendly rattler tuh end yuh troubles! They's still Gawd knows whut the hail in them mountains. Git in and eat, now.'

The whole crew was at the table, Grits spooning out stew and cutting hunks of panbread. They looked up.

'Hah!' snorted Grits. 'I told yuh gals I'd shoot mah own danged hands off iffen the smell a my stew din' bring her runnin' back! Alleluia! I hate it when folk jest disappear.'

'Been doing a little exploring,' I said, fighting the give-away grin I'd been wearing all the way home.

Suzanna smiled, a lazy twinkle that started at her mouth and idled through to the ultraviolet spangle of her eyes. 'Y' see, Angel? She ain't pinched the family jewels. Angel here's been speculating about the honesty of your reputation, Typewriter. Come and sit down. Here.'

I sat next to her. She sniffed, smiled suddenly and said, 'You been up the hill? I can smell the sage on you. Where'd you go?'

'Up to the falls.' I reckoned I'd keep vague about Me Old China till I could be on my own with Suzanna, but Grievous thumped the table and hollered:

'Goddammit! I got shit fer brains! It's today, ain't it – that Injun woman said fer us to go up there today fer a ceremony. Only all th' other stuff goin' on drove it clean outta my head. She really wanted us to go – didja meet her, Typewriter?'

'Yeah,' I said. 'It was the Butterfly Ceremony. Today's

the day for the vision of butterflies. It's supposed to be a good sign. They'll be here in three weeks. We did the – ceremony. She said to say Wotcher, Suzanna, said she'd be calling by real soon.'

Suzanna smiled. 'No wonder you're late,' she drawled. 'You got some luck, Typewriter. I didn't come across Me Old China till I'd been here nigh on a year. She'd been watchin' us all that time and we never knew. Finally figured we were OK and so she made the meeting. She don't change words with no one unless she wants to. But, damn! *You* jest got here yesterday and happen on her, and happen on the Butterfly Ceremony! That's some honour! Me, I never got to do none of the ceremonies with her till two years back. Time just flies, don't it, what with the crazy weed and all?'

Her eyes met and challenged mine. My grin burst into laughter and she laughed with me, while Grievous cussed about how she'd missed it, and a year was a hell of a time to wait, just supposin' we was even still here in a year.

'There's other ceremonies,' said Suzanna. 'Me Old China can always find a legend from her people to celebrate something. Only she always chooses who can join her.'

'Ain't that the truth?' said Mira with a warm smile. 'I got slung out on my butt when the moon went from black cherries to leaf-fall. It had to be you, Lucille, all by yourself, on account of your damn red hair which nature never meant it that way.'

Lariat Lucille laughed. 'You're wrong, honey. I do believe it was my eyes got me there, Rainbow-Wings said they held the promise of springtime!'

'Well, I got the dancing horses,' said Suzanna with a dreamy grin. 'Was about the time the storm clouds come over. Gawd, the rain was like a thousand kisses . . .'

'Who is this Indian woman?' said Angel, uneasily.

'Of course, you and Mercedes wouldn't know a damn thing about her. Makes me feel old, Angel, when I think how long I've been here. And maybe I'm just that little bit wiser for knowing Me Old China. I kin tell you what I know the way she told it to me. Yeah, let me tell you a story,' said Suzanna. 'Are you all listening? Good, then I'll begin.

'Once upon a time, before you were born, or me either, there was a tribe of Indians lived in this valley, Kimama. The men rushed around fighting and collecting horses, and the women ran the show. Wise women made every decision, and that's the way it was and always had been until the white men came. The tribe took to the hills and hid, but you cain't hide minnows from ravening sharks. Alwiz was the worst kinda sharks come out first in th' old West, sniffing fer blood and damn near crazy at the scent of it. Jerking off a rain of hot lead's easier than talking for some, specially the kind got nothing but an asswipe between their ears. So these no-account hombres done what they could by way of wiping out the tribe, only they reckoned without the women. Eight braves bit the dust and got strung up on trees as a warning to the rest. To make it worse – if it could be – they got strung up on the branches of a sacred grove, and the rest of the grove chopped down for firewood.

'Next thing they know, the Indians have come to make peace: all the women came down, acting up, and the murdering white-trash vultures had th' idea their luck was in. Their luck had run clean out. In the morning, there was twenty sleeping rolls stained with blood, and only one white man alive, the cook, Charlie. He'd been laying with Me Old China's mother, only he said it wasn't right and he didn't hold with none of it. Not the killing, nor layin' with a woman didn't want to.'

'I remember Me Old China talkin' about Charlie!' broke in Grievous. 'Didn't he go live with the Indians? She called him Charlie Cock-Knee, wasn't it?'

'He was from London, England,' said Suzanna, nodding. 'The tribe liked him, and Me Old China's mother liked him particularly. He called himself a sparrow, and they took him in as one of them. Birds were sacred to them, all flying things meant good magic. I guess it's him she picked up her English from . . . blamed if I can understand half a what she comes out with. It's a bad story aside from Charlie. Most of the women who'd lain with the white men got disease, and the tribe felt there was a curse on the place. Just split up and drifted away. Only Me Old China left now. She keeps an eye on the place, waiting, she says. Waiting for what, I said? Waiting, me old darling, she says, ain't that good enough?'

'Seemed like a good kinda woman when I met her – aw, hell, the best,' said Lariat Lucille, blowing a lasso of smoke to the ceiling.

'Very friendly,' said Mira, in her deep east-European drawl.

'Mighty hospitable,' said Roo with a glimmer of a smile.

Me, Suzanna, Lucille, Roo and Mira – Me Old China must have had quite a few *ceremonies* up in the hills. There was the same delighted I'm-keeping-it-to-myself grin sitting pretty on all our faces. I don't like to kiss and tell . . . and neither did any one of these sun-bronzed amazons. But I knew, they knew, and we all knew. A mighty fine memory, these ceremonies with Me Old China.

And it was more than not kissing and telling. Something had shifted in me that afternoon by the waterfall, something more powerful than language could ever get hold of. Different from the blindfold cliff-leap freedom of my fly-away new name; some sleeping strength in me had been unshackled when I didn't even know it was there, had been there, all the time.

'Seems we should drink her health,' said Suzanna with an awkward graciousness, strolling from the table to break out a fresh bottle of bourbon. 'We're gonna be needin' every ounce of luck and magic there is for this venture.'

THIRTEEN

The bourbon glowed smooth as an Acapulco gold sunset, and we shifted into the big room to sprawl easy on Suzanna's huge chairs and couch. Suzanna said something quietly to Angel, and when I looked up next the huge oak door to the office was shut tight behind them. Mira, Roo, Lucille and Grits started a game of poker.

'I love tah watch yuh blind bluffing,' crooned Roo, squeezing Mira's hand.

Grievous and Assassina sat by me. Some of Mercedes's wildfire seemed tamed: I asked them how the day had gone. Mercedes's dark eyes flashed.

'My kind of day,' she said. 'We burned out the west pasture. Santa Maria y Jesus! I never knew starting a fire could be so complicated – when I did that fire in La Valkeria I had no mind of it ever going out.'

'If I hadn't ben carryin' th' kerosene,' said Grievous, 'we'd a ben eatin' roasted earth fer the rest of our lives. Yuh dingbat!'

There was a pleasant comradeship in the punches they feinted at each other.

'Yuh see,' said Grievous, 'yuh start a fire without yuh taste the wind first, yuh got more problems than a three-legged woman givin' birth. Yuh gotta set a while and see how the wind is dancin', then lay yuh snake-trail of powder so she bites it with yuh.'

'What a sight!' breathed Mercedes. 'I love a blaze, and the smell of it! But to see flames licking along a path you've made, like a dog you'd trained to do fancy tricks! You're a fuckin' artist, Grievous.'

'Thank you, dear,' said Grievous, flattered as hell. 'You're not so bad yourself.'

Suzanna stalked into the room, a scarlet flush rising in

her neck. Without a word she scooped up the bourbon bottle, strode back into her office and slammed the door closed.

'You're playing blind, *camarada mia*,' growled Mira, to which Roo shrugged, grinned and said:

'Maybe I got a fancy hand here, Mira . . . maybe yuh better watch that precious dutch straight yuh love so much.'

'What's she sayin' to Angel?' muttered Mercedes, edgy as a cayuse sensing a scorpion.

'Don't yuh fret none, precious,' soothed Grievous. 'Whatever she says, our lives gonna be smoother here on in.'

'You have a lot of faith in Suzanna,' grudged Assassina, diving her predatory mouth at the glass of firewater.

'Damn right I do! Ah alwiz wuz a loner till I met Suzanna,' said Grievous. 'Never ridden alone since – she has a mighty comfortin' presence. Why, I recall the time we was holed up in Halligan's Hayloft, back in Zekiah Swamp, and a pair of saddlebags full a greenbacks hotter 'n the devil's britches snugglin' up between th' pair of us. Suzanna finally figgered tuh git us done up as a pair of tramp whores jest come across th' damn bags an' we handed them in tuh the bank fuh the *ree*-ward. We walked outta that no-'count burg with new hosses, clean money and a half-dozen offers most wimmin down on they luck couldn't a refused. Yuh gotta adapt, said Suzanna: shee-it! Iffen we'd stuck tuh bein' bank robbers we'd a ben feedin' the desert vultures come sun-up. As it wuz, our hides remained clean as a angel's asshole, and we wuz richer for it.'

'I hate to compromise,' said Assassina, breathing deep.

'Yiii-ih, Mercedes, and thass why y'all wound up in Pulque for five years, when me an' Suzanna's walked outta most raps been due to us,' said Grievous.

'What did you do to get in Pulque?' I asked Mercedes Assassina, by way of conversation.

Who has not heard the name of Pulque? The rathole of hell in the bloodless heart of New Mexico! The jail where they shift all the wrongdoers judged too evil and dangerous to do time anywhere else. The snakepit, piranha pool of jails in a country that prides itself on calabooses close enough to the spirit of the Inquisition to take the heart out of the profanest reptile ever made his pact with Beelzebub! And Assassina was a woman. Usually a good-looking woman could bring lecherous tears to the eyes of the most hard-baked judge. But she'd wound up at Pulque inside the waiting-room of death – and survived!

'Well,' said Assassina, surveying the half-inch of brown incandescence swirling the bottom of her glass. She downed it and leaned forwards. 'I was born to a good family, Typewriter. So good there was no courting for the daughters. You married the man chosen for you by your father. My father was a man rich on the crow-plucked bones of peasants; my mother lay on silk sheets and wept for her home in Valencia: she was ill, we were told, ill or giving birth. She had seven daughters: I was the seventh. My father wanted a boy. So she was a failed woman, and died with the eighth child, a sickly grub of a boy – but a *boy*, a *man* in the making, my brother, for whom the sun rose and set . . . Gaaaah!

'And then my father said he had made a match for me. I should be grateful for an old man, old as my father, and I was *so lucky* that a man should want me, the seventh daughter, with so little inheritance. I swear, no bride ever wept as I did. My *husband* – God curse him! – had ideas about this young wife. I was just a woman's body to live out his dreams. Dreams? The man's brain was a sick nightmare! I can't talk about what he had done to me. And three weeks later, I torched the house when he was so drunk his breath would have lit with a spark!

'Fool that I was, I stayed to dance around the flames. It made me feel clean. And so – Pulque. If I had shed one tear for my dead husband in front of that judge, I would have been free. But my tears were frozen, it was only for myself I could have cried.'

'Suzanna read the case,' said Grievous. 'Figured here was a woman who'd been done more wrong than she'd done – that's when we decided to spring Assassina. Longest job I ever ben on with Suzanna. Most expensive, too. We din' read about it till two years later, and it took us three tuh spread the right bribes around. It wuz fuckin' close, Typewriter.'

We sat back. Mercedes's histrionics suddenly seemed to have a whole thorn thicket of reason behind. OK, I'd been tarred bitch and ballbreaker when I stood up my beau in the interests of what I liked to call my career – but I knew these American-Spanish patriarchs and the way they disposed of women's flesh, their daughters' lives, like they were playing roulette.

'Skip!' whooped Lariat Lucille, slapping her cards on the table. 'Call yuh one and call yuh all – dutch straight!'

'Waaall,' hazarded Roo. 'Take it back if yuh wanna save yuh hide, Lucille . . .'

Mira smiled. 'Wang-doodle and y'all owe me your lives for the next ten years,' she breathed, and spread out the kind of flush got Diamond Jim's hide perforated like swiss cheese.

As she spoke, the office door was flung open, and Suzanna came in, drawing Angel by the hand.

'Hey, folks,' she said, and we all looked at her. 'I want you to meet my daughter – Angel Star.'

FOURTEEN

If music be the food of love, then Suzanna's face was playing the finest symphony ever heard. If the silence of the mind is the silence of the earth, then all of us,

Grievous, Mira, Roo, Lucille, Assassina, Grits and me, became continents and mountain ranges at that moment.

Suzanna sat on a wide low sofa with Angel beside her, that hypnotized look she wore as happy as I'd ever see it.

'Grievous,' she said, forcing her voice to come out even, 'pour us all a drink. Whatthehell. Nearest to celebrating we'll be this year.'

Grievous poured.

'Guess I have some explaining to do,' said Suzanna, winding her fabulous arm round Angel's shoulders. 'Guess y'all thought I didn't have no family nor blood alive. Lemme tell y' about Rooster Rudd Prink – if it's OK with you, honey?'

Angel nodded against her shoulder. Closed those insane blue eyes in what looked like ecstasy.

'Chequered past? Mine's a tapestry, folks,' said Suzanna, flinging one leg over the other. 'I done a little showbiz here 'n there – as Typewriter here can testify – and then I was at a loose end. Met this fancy-pants silver-tongue showman, smooth as my daddy – Rooster Rudd Prink and his Amazing Travelling Circus. I was flipped outta my head enough to fall for the twenty-carat bullshit – you know how it is when you get adrift from your life. Well, I was so lost and lonely I got friendly with him, enough to forget my dreams, and, to cut it short, I had me a baby same time as a rap from Tucson caught up with me. The baby was born in jail, and I done my best to follow her then on – it was Angel here. Goddam, when I think of her daddy: it was endangering the soul of my boot to wipe it on shit like him! But out of it all comes Angel. My child. I've always said this here valley held my family, and when we bust Angel out – I knew it.'

'Waall, I'll be ding-dong-daddio-ed!' burst in Grievous. 'I have detected a change in yuh since Angel here showed up, and danged ef I'd ever have put y' alongside of maternal instinct!'

Lariat Lucille's golden teeth shone in her smile. She

57

raised her glass. 'Suzanna, it makes me easier hearin' that. I thought, truth t' tell, yuh'd gone soft fer a pretty face – hell, no lies about it, Roo and Mira thought the same dam thang! 'Course yuh'd flip blind fuh yuh own long-lost babby! Hot damn and shit me easy! Here's tuh yuh both!'

'And being as how I've found this little hell-raiser here – goddam, I love you, honey,' said Suzanna, kissing Angel's blonde head in the crook of her arm, 'we all oughtta have a serious parley about what things are going down in this valley. Kimama!'

She raised her glass and we all said *Kimama*, like it was the word of God.

Suzanna untwined herself from Angel, who flopped across her lap, sucking her thumb. Suzanna kept one hand on her cheek, but for the rest, she was Suzanna LaReine, whose name was whispered in awe and terror east of Kimama.

'We done good today,' she said. 'I seen that fire – *molto bueno*, Grievous *mia*, Assassina, Roo. Me and Lucille and Angel got the horses well west, beyond the smoke and the terror. I reckon, hate the danged idea tho' I do, we gotta create the same kinda hell right across – this jackass punkins, Mr Darknell van Doon, gonna need some serious persuasion to get th' idea of pasturin' his cattle away from here. Let's hope we kin do it.'

'And what if we don't?' Roo's voice cut into the pensive silence like a razor.

'If we don't – I don't wanna hear about don't,' said Lariat Lucille, knotting her hand into a fist to be reckoned with.

'Me neither,' said Grievous, shifting her boots on the floor like the cellar below was on fire.

'Roo's right – we hafta consider that remote possibility,' said Suzanna, her fingers still moving through Angel's hair. 'If we don't – there is land west and north of here. But I'll lay odds we kin hold the bastards back, for our

lifetimes, anyhow. And I got me a new incentive –
goddam, let's drink to the new generation.'

Angel removed her thumb from her lips and straightened up beside her long-lost mother, suddenly grown up.
Side by side, you could note the resemblance: a firmness
of the jaw and an invincible spirited flash of the eyes.
Rooster Rudd Prink could be held accountable for the
sullen set of Angel's jaw, tho' Suzanna could have done
that all by herself on a bad day, I guessed.

We drank.

'I figure Me Old China will mosey by the next few days,'
said Suzanna, tossing her shot the way of all flesh. "Till
then, we carry on torching the pasture, and keeping the
grullas outta trouble. And goodnight, ladies.'

The crew shifted out of the house. Angel went upstairs
with Suzanna, and pretty soon I heard the hush slam of a
door that means privacy. I shifted out on the porch with
Fingerbone, and lit a cheroot.

'She keeps me guessin',' said the rot-toothed ancient.
'Who'd ever a thought she had a natural-born child? Not
me, fer one. Twenty years I follow that woman, near as,
and now she got herself a damn jailbird baby! Hev a drink,
Typewriter.'

I applied my lips to her bottle. The rotgut tasted almost
sweet in the pitchblende night.

'Here's to you, Fingerbone,' I muttered.

The ancient lungs gave vent to what might have been a
laugh.

FIFTEEN

I sweated awake early from a weird dream, slept again
uneasily and landed back in the same place, where the
colours were too vivid, the lines too sharp, and everything
was etched with the shimmering precision you see in a

landscape before a twister hits. In the dream, I had left Suzanna's house at night for a walk and suddenly I found myself in a town full of dazzling white houses, hectic green lawns and little alleys lined with trees where the solid shadows lay like they'd been painted. It was daytime in the town, under a harsh blue sky. There was a feeling of moneyed leisure in the place, but the streets were uncannily empty where there should have been petti-coated belles strolling along with parasols and dandified young men with swagger canes tipping their hats. Silence, and then an ear-shattering explosion as a rough plains wagon came careering out of nowhere straight at me, wheels thundering, dust roaring, whip cracking and a jeering *Yeeeeeeeee – hah*! I jumped aside and leaped on the running board. The driver was a huge unshaven pot of greed and liquor, and set about booting me off . . .

That was when I woke again.

The second dream was the same, only this time I knew to run away down alleys too narrow for the wagon, and wound up back in Kimama, just this side of the pass, walking for ever to get back to the house. And there was Suzanna, and everyone, and never even noticed I'd gone. My heart was racing with real fear that I never would get back. And that for sure I never wanted to leave again.

I didn't wish to risk a third visit to that nightmare, so I got up and went outside. Fingerbone was asleep on the porch, twitched one red eye open, shrugged back to sleep. I walked down the field and through the trees as the sun was rising, streaking platinum along the clouds, burning the thin veil of mist off the valley floor wide as an uncharted ocean.

I met a crazy woman once, who read dreams in Champagne, Illinois. It paid for her liquor. I tried to recall what she'd said – something about everyone in your dream was you, and every place you saw you'd either seen or you'd be going there some day. It made no sense to me. But that feeling of panic swept back as I looked over the valley: I really didn't want to leave here, and most everything in my life I've really wanted has been snatched away from me just when I was beginning to feel easy with it.

I built a smoke, still half in my bad dream, and was mighty glad when Roo's voice hailed me, and she came and sat by me.

'You're settin' in my chair, Typewriter!' she joshed me. 'I always set here about this time and git myself acquainted with the day.'

I shifted over and we smoked in silence.

'Gonna be busy, Typewriter,' she said finally. 'You want to ride with me and Lucille? We gotta check the pass, and I figure we'll be soothin' the grullas.'

'Well, OK,' I said. I liked the idea of a hard ride in this fresh day.

'Well, let's git goin',' said Roo, setting off for the bunkhouse.

Grievous was groaning for coffee, and grinned at me.

'Slummin' it down with the girls, huh?'

'I figured there's family business going on up at the house,' I said, taking a steaming cup from the pot.

'Waall,' said Grievous, pumping water over her head. 'Me and Mercedes reckon it's back to fire-raisin'. You?'

'Roo said to ride up to the pass with her and Lucille, maybe look out for the grullas on the way.'

'Naah!' said Lucille. 'Suzanna and Angel'll do that. Both of them nuts about horses. Most human thing about Angel Star.'

Mira stretched and picked up a sledgehammer like it was a feather.

'I'll fix that fence on the winter corral,' she said. 'Make me believe we'll be here another winter, eh?'

I was amazed at the change in Dawn, my mare: between the good air, the grass and Angel's grooming, she was glossy and frisky and we cannoned across the plain. The beauty of Kimama had hit me even when I slumped in, dead beat, behind Grievous. Now I revelled in the sheer sweep of the land, and the pale-gold early sun on the peaks.

We stopped after a couple of hours' solid riding, and looked back. The buildings were out of sight, but in the distance we could see a plume of dark smoke: Mercedes and Grievous had made good time. I liked Lucille and Roo's company, though we hardly exchanged a word, beyond one of them pointing out some of the bizarre clusters of rock.

'Grievous!' said Roo, as we passed a monolith clumped like a fist; 'Fingerbone!' said Lucille, laughing at a great orange chimney blasted black at its tip. And then we slowed as the path became steeper, and I recognized the forbidding bluffs I'd struggled through – Jesus! was it only three days before?

For the last bit we led the horses, then let them loose to pick up what little grass there was. There was a change in the air – more than just the cool of height; the rocks were a sunless grey, a sluggish washed-out yellow.

'The earth gets sour round here,' said Lucille. 'I hate this fuckin' place. Me Old China said something really bad happened here – like, so bad she won't give details – with her people long before the white men came. It put a curse on the land, and the curse spreads all the way down to the plain beyond.'

'The homesteaders I met seemed to have some kind of blight,' I said, recalling the exhausted hopeless family. 'And getting through this pass is like shitting needles.'

'Something in the earth,' said Roo. 'Ground's firm up to here, and th' other side's like quicksand or one of them godawful stews Fingerbone makes when she kin slide by Grits and start messin' up the stove.'

'Jeez!' said Lucille. 'And she says she cooked fer Calamity Jane and if it was good enough for her, what're we belly-achin' about?'

'Belly-achin' about achin' bellies!' said Roo, and her laugh rang in the barren air.

The path ran two ways: one over the pass and we took the other. It stopped at a blank wall of rock.

'Like a fuckin' door, ain't it, Typewriter?' said Lucille. 'Me Old China says it was put there by magic to seal off Kimama, and it did until a landslide knocked that path through below. We gotta climb it.'

'Ain't as bad as it looks,' said Roo, slapping my shoulder, and eeling through a needle-thin crack. I followed, and found myself in a narrow chimney of rock towering up so high the sky didn't appear bigger than a ten-cent piece.

The rock was spider-webbed with cracks and up we went, mostly able to brace our backs and knees against the roughness. I was soaked in a cold sweat by the time I was at the top. There was no rock higher on the range above the pass, and the wind stung my face. We were standing on top of the giant stone door, and could see for miles. The horses were a shimmer of brown and gold dots on the plain; the distant fire was like the smoke from a spent match. I narrowed my eyes in the dazzling light.

'Is that the house?'

'Yup. Suzanna built it there when she first come here: this is the only place in the valley you can see it from. The idea was we could light a beacon here if there was real trouble from the east. Goddam! We could use some a that magic the Indians knew about and we've never had a sense or sight of. We'd be sittin' pretty if we could git another of these suckers against the west!'

We lay flat at the edge of the rock: the path I had nearly died on was a tattered muddy ribbon below, and I could see the hopeless homestead like a pile of boards away on the scrubby plain, and then – nothing, till your eye fetched up against the blur of distant mountains. We were at the edge of the world.

SIXTEEN

'Waaa-all, I reckon we've done all a woman can,' said Suzanna, as we rode back from the scorched western acres. It was the day before Mr Darknell van Doon was due. We'd drug a number of bones out of the trees and river, and Me Old China had arranged them in the form of carrion birds and snakes, to symbolize that No Arms Hackmore and his bloodthirsty buddies would be back, if they'd been there in the first place.

'Chin up, duchess,' said Me Old China, grinning like a crazy woman. 'There's a lot more we can do if Flash Britches don't get the idea he ain't welcome.'

'Like what?' said Suzanna, puffing away to keep her cheroot alive.

'That's for me to know and you to find out, darling!' she flung over her shoulder, galloping ahead with a stream of blood-curdling whoops and what was probably cussing.

'She means magic,' said Grievous. 'Feathers and bones and animal hair an stuff – ain't gonna be shit against fuckin' civilization and syndicates.'

'Heck alone knows what'll do it then,' said Lucille. 'She told us that rock in th' eastern pass was raised and dropped there by *hummin'*. *Hummin'*, fer chrissake! See that dip in the middle of the plain, where that lake is – she says that's where the rock flew up from like a skylark offa its eggs!'

'Gimme dynamite any day,' said Grievous.

'Yew kin crack glass singin',' said Roo. 'Wuz a woman in the Wild West Show done that. Mighty expensive – mighty impressive – ever'thin' went from beer glasses to eyeglasses. We had tah let her go after a while, one town she put out every window in the saloon when one of them cowboys got a mite too fresh.'

'Sheee-it!' said Grievous. 'I wish I'd seen that.'

'Horseshit!' jeered Suzanna. 'Hey – whassa matter with them two?'

'Jest bitchin' and arguin' agin,' said Grievous, looking to where Mercedes and Angel were jostling each other. 'You'd a thought they'd a straightened out some. Mercedes done good fire-raisin', almost made her crack her face to smilin'. And goddam! Angel ain't got nuthin' tuh fire off her mouth about, knowin' you're her mother, I'd a thought.'

'Grievous, it don't appear to have helped none. What-the-hell did I expect – someone to comfort my old age?'

True, Angel had relapsed into moods like a sky full of rain clouds, and silences spitting louder than thunder. For the last week, almost. And she wouldn't sleep at the house.

'Hell, I tried to get her to part them angry lips yesterday evening,' said Suzanna, shrugging. 'She didn't want to know. Said she didn't have nothing to say to me. Damn! If I'd a raised her I'd a cracked her head . . . Somethin's brewin'. She's got plenty to say. One thing she never got from me, nor that bedbug poppa of hers – we kin both lie straight-faced. Her face's like an open book.'

We mooched back to the house. Plenty of time to sort out Angel Star after we sorted out Mr Darknell van Doon and his shit-eating syndicate.

That evening round supper there was an edginess could have been down to what would happen the next day and could have been down to Angel's face, which it was blank, her eyes on her plate. She ignored everything that could have brought her into talking, even the horses. Finally, the words petered out around her.

'Dammit, honey!' exploded Suzanna, thundering her fist on the table so the silverware, glassware and plates did a tap dance. 'Don't sit there chewing your food like it was shit and ashes! You got something on your mind, spill it out!'

65

Angel swallowed and stared at her. The kind of look to send your fingers twitching around the butt of your hawg-leg.

'You think you're really something, don't you, Suzanna LaReine?' Her voice was flat as a stagnant pond, and about as pleasant.

'Aw, sheee-it!' snarled Grievous, bunching her fists up. 'Angel! Watch your damn mouth!'

'You all think she's really something, doncha?' Angel's eyes stabbed all round the table, and her lips twisted like they had live wires inside them. Suzanna's neck was crimson, with a vein standing out like a poison snake ready to strike.

'I been thinkin',' said Angel, forcing the words out. 'You say you're *my mother*. I don't see you in nearly twenty years, and suddenly, you got to bust me outta jail. So I got to be grateful. Which I was to breathe air again, but I gotta be grateful to *you*. Cuz I coulda busted my own way outta that piss 'n plaster outhouse jail any time I had a mind to, being as the sheriff was sweet on me. But I wouldn't stoop that low. And I thought you were something, Suzanna, I thought you were a fuckin' guardian angel, sent to save me. What a fool I bin. Why'd you bust me out? Make up for twenty years you couldn't give a sheep's fart about me? Make yourself feel good?'

'Go on,' said Suzanna, her voice like a steel-coated glacier. 'All this is real educational.'

Angel drew in a breath big enough to blow the house down. Out on that breath came spewing a torrent:

'So we come back here, to happy valley, where Queen Suzanna holds court, being as she's decided it that way and everybody else round here got gopher guts and reckons that's just fine and dandy with them. Me too till I started thinking! You got a different face for everyone you meet, bitch, and none of 'em look pretty to me! You got some nuts idea you can stop Darknell van Doon with a bit

66

of burnt scrub and a crazy Injun woman who'll open her legs for anyone?'

No doubt she had plenty more, only that minute, Me Old China leaped from her chair clear across the table and crouched in front of her, about space enough between their faces to slide a piece of paper through. And Me Old China had her bone knife claiming squatter's rights on Angel's throat. Angel didn't turn a hair.

'OK, scum,' said Me Old China. 'Out of respect to your mother – Suzanna, you want to see a scalp or you want me to cut this mile of dirt out of her mouth? It's your flesh and blood.'

'No,' said Suzanna.

Me Old China took one leap backwards like a cat, and sat like a copper statue that had never moved at all. Only her eyes were fixed on Angel and it didn't take a whole heap of intelligence to read that look.

'Never forget Suzanna saved your life, walking shit,' she said.

Angel screamed like a mare with a thorn tied under her saddle, flung to her feet and blazed:

'Another thing I have to be *grateful* for? She gave me birth – I was never asked, did I want her for a mother. She broke me out of jail – I didn't even know her name. One word from her and you leave me alive – did you ask *me*? You can rot in hell, you swelled-up bloodsucker! You're no mother to me! A mother is the person who raises you and cares for you, not some power-crazy she-wolf who rides out of nowhere and claims you after twenty years like you were a parcel she'd just dropped some place! You're a fuckin' monster!'

Lucille was behind her and I heard the click of a gun.

'Shut it, but *good*,' she said. 'Suzanna, I'm locking her up for the night. And tomorrow. We don't need bughouse blues on top of the mountain of troubles we got already.'

It was no question, but Suzanna nodded. Angel raised her arms and let her hands hang in midair like she didn't give a damn. As she passed Suzanna she spat on her shoulder. The screen door slammed.

I leaned over and wiped the spit from her shirt. The pain and rage in her eyes burned as she looked at me.

'Thanks, Typewriter,' she said.

SEVENTEEN

'Waaa-aall, let's go sit a while,' said Suzanna. The air at the table was like walking on splinters. She poured cold beer.

'So – tomorrow,' she said, and ran through the plan.

I had been watching Assassina so she wouldn't notice. She'd enjoyed every bit of what had gone on. Her eyes were ablaze with a grim satisfaction and her full lips were set in a bow of triumph. What the hell had she and Angel been so busy talking about as we rode back? She was the only woman in the room who didn't seem in the least surprised at the whole thing.

Late that evening, Suzanna beckoned me into the office.

'Bourbon, Typewriter? I alwiz think clearer through them fumes,' she said. She looked older and sad. We drank.

'You know what that was about?' she said. 'I'll tell you.' She sat heavily.

'When we busted Angel out, I was so proud. Finally done something for my child once she'd turned out as law-abiding as me. Figured she needed me. I was so – never felt so – when I saw her face, I just wanted to hold her and say, Hey, child, it's OK now, you got your natural momma, things'll be fine here on in. But I couldn't just tell her outright. You know the way I was raised? Church folk doing good to a poor orphan?'

'Yeah,' I said. It hurt me to hear such pain from a woman so fine.

'Waaa-all, Angel had that, only worse, seeing as how they thought they were saving the soul of a jailbird's child. She got spun a high-falutin' tale about a sainted pop and momma died of swamp fever and asked her foster parents to raise her like their own, with their dyin' breath. Then she finds herself growing wild and can't do a natural thing to please 'em. It ain't in her blood, all that sanctimoaning and alleluia. And then when she held up that store, and got herself jailed, she was hoping to come out and start again and be decent and be a credit to the folks who raised her.'

'She tell you all this?'

'Every word, the night I told her I was her mom, and we got real close. She's been chewing it over and come up with bitter spit – for me. An outlaw for a mother and a no-good son of a bitch I didn't even marry or love or stay with for a father! So she reckons it's my bad blood made her go wrong. I ain't nothing but a disaster happened to her.'

'I don't get it. Entirely,' I said, feeling the worst was yet to come.

'The first night she was back here,' said Suzanna, refilling her glass, 'we had a party. A little drunk, a big drunk – honey, I wanted to celebrate! We were all whooping it up out here, Maloof got her old fiddle out and Mira was singing so as to drown it out, hell, we got rowdy. Everyone knew it was more than just a jail bust for me, and Assassina was sulking like a horntoad missed a luscious fly, being as we hadn't done nothing so fancy for her. Anyways, we were all stomping around and having a good time, and I got to hugging Angel. I ain't the type, but I was just trying to figure out how the hell to say I was her mom.

'I did it all wrong. I told her I was real fond of her, and what with the out-of-the-blue bust and me hugging her, she got the wrong idea – y'know what I mean? You know what I mean. Not mother love. She'd always had a yen for women, all her life, and real confused about not having nor wanting a regular beau. Just like me, aside from that one son of a bitch, Rooster Rudd Prink, and his devil's good looks. I didn't know right off she'd taken it that way. I took her into the office where we could be private and explain why this old outlaw thought she was the cutest thing the sun shines on. She wanted me so bad, Typewriter, I just couldn't say it out, just then. I just said I was a little drunk and it wasn't that way for me. Shit!'

Suzanna gulped her drink.

'Y'understand what I'm saying? Goddam, you always understand what I'm saying, right from Coolee. I watched you walk away from me then, and I knew you the minute you drug up here with Grievous and Assassina. I knew you were the bone-headed loner who'd saved my hide back there right at the beginning of my career, after you'd sworn to button your lip. But the only way I could tell you was showing you that folder. I ain't shit at coming out with stuff when it's real important to me.'

I nodded. Reckoned I understood. Give me a sheet of paper and I'll write a love letter; face-to-face I get mighty conversational about such stuff as the state of the nation and the weather for the time of year – stuff I don't go hog-wild about. I get real loquacious about all kinds of crap, but I *love* you? Sticks in my throat like a whalebone. I figure my heart goes straight to my head and misses my mouth out on the way.

'Angel,' I said. I wanted to hear all of this.

'So,' said Suzanna, laying her head back on the chair like she was bushed, 'Angel decides I am one loose, mean, teasing old bitch full a shit – that's how come she was so wild when you first seen her. Taking pot shots at any blade of grass had the nerve to shift in the wind, and wishing it was me. I thought it would be better after I told her I was her mother. It ain't better. She don't want to believe it, even. It's bad, Typewriter. Whaddya think?'

'I think – give her time. Give her tomorrow to cool off

70

and think. Talk to her like you've talked to me. And if you have to, let her go. She's a grown woman, and only a half of her came from you. You don't even know each other.'

'Half me, half her crowing pop. And years of preaching from do-good sanctifiers. Hell, I had all that in my own childhood after the fire. You know all about that from what you read. If ever I'd hoped for a god, that hope died when I was going on fourteen. Seemed like guilt and repentance for stuff I hadn't even dreamed of was God's way. I felt I was just naturally wicked. I guess you're right.'

We walked upstairs. I got one of those flashes where I have to speak – and a sudden sense of danger.

'Sleep in with me?' I said.

She sighed.

'Yeah,' she said.

I held her close all night. Woke when she shouted in her sleep, stroked her hair as if she was a baby. Woke once to find her weeping like her heart was broken.

Sunrise and she was Suzanna LaReine again, *don't need nobody*, swung her legs out of the bed and sat up. Then she turned and looked at me.

'I won't say a word,' I said, and meant it. She smiled ruefully.

'Thanks,' she said, and left the room to face the day.

When I got up, I looked into her room. What I saw made my blood run cold as a melting icicle. Gleaming in the middle of her pillow, right where her head would have been, was a cut-throat stiletto standing stiff and deadly as a rattler poised for the kill.

My heart jolted and when I breathed there was pain. If I hadn't spoken on instinct the night before, if Suzanna hadn't slept in with me . . . her blood would be staining the pillow right now, her heartbeat stopped for ever. I shut my eyes for an instant. I had only just found her – and could have lost her on the tip of this murderous blade.

I clenched my teeth, bunched my fists and cursed the hand that had turned against her.

As I slid the steel from the cotton into my pocket I swore vengeance for this outrage, this blasphemy. When the time came I would be ready.

Meanwhile there was business to go through with Mr Darknell van Doon and his threat on our way of life.

And then there would be more than a little explaining to do.

EIGHTEEN

We had set the backdrop as fancy as a theatre-play for Mr Darknell van Doon. Only we weren't aiming for a long run. Way we saw it was, first he'd ride past the burnt-out fields and get the sense something wasn't right, and between there and the house he'd have himself some troublesome thoughts. Then we aimed to confound him further.

Suzanna had forced Mary Maloof Fingerbone out of her kippered threads, into a bath, then out of the bath and into a sprigged muslin dress Grits was saving to be buried in. She had then plaited up Fingerbone's long grey hair and wound it round her head with fancy grips. To a mudslide of cussing, she'd confiscated her flask and given her a glass like ordinary folks drink lemonade out of. Finally, Suzanna had put all her old stogies away for safekeeping, ramming a corncob pipe into her hand when Fingerbone dug her heels right in on no smoke all day. She had hung on to her twelve-bore like grim death as well and finally consented to hiding it under a woollen shawl worn like a regular old lady rising seventy years.

The idea was Darknell van Doon would see a dear little old granmaw rocking herself on the home-sweet-home porch and get himself all of a lather about how we'd handled the cut-throat hustlers he believed to be infesting the hills. He'd be near shittin' his fine pants for what he might find inside the house. Fingerbone had sworn on the Good Book not to open her sewer-pipe mouth.

'I'll be ******* deaf and double-******* dumb – now leave me be!' she grated out, spat and plumped down in the rocker.

Grits dumped a mess of knitting on her lap.

'Granmaw got to appear to make herself useful,' she said. 'I had a granmaw once and her lips never touched liquor, and her hands was never idle.'

If looks could burn the breath and blood out of a body, Grits would have been a heap of cinders on the bleached boards. As it was, she cackled at the fury on Fingerbone's scrubbed face and went indoors. You gotta eat good when trouble comes knocking, and she was cooking a banquet fit for a king.

Around noon, Fingerbone hissed, 'Cowpoke linen-britches is here – in a goddam surrey!'

'Not another word from you!' said Suzanna.

We looked at each other. The idea was I was her financial partner, one of those eccentric eastern women with all the power of untold dollars behind them.

A prosperous voice was heard hallooing and we made our entrance.

'Anyone home, folks? Good mornin' tew yew, Miz Comstock!'

'Mr van Doon,' she said.

'Good day to you, Miz Comstock, and – ma'am,' he said, heaving himself from the surrey and raising a store-bought stetson a mile high. 'I brung mah liddle gal along with me – mah wife, Lulumae – this here's Miz Comstock I told you all about. Figure me Lulumae got herself a mite curious about yew, Miz Comstock!'

'Ah do have to keep an aaaah awn *mah man*!' fluted Lulumae, teetering to the ground with the help of his flesh-filled sleeve. She extended one lace-gloved hand. I swear it was pearl-buttoned six to an inch all the way to the elbow. The rest of Lulumae van Doon was ribboned and laced and smocked and pleated and tucked and embroidered and braided and trimmed and appliquéd and french-knotted like a seamstress was trying to show all the tricks of the trade on the one dress. Her waist was pulled in tight as the neck of a sack of gold-dust, then her skirts shot out over petticoats so stiff you could have skied down them. She had the kind of face that has never willingly been in full sunlight – 'mah man' held a silk-fringed parasol to shade her now.

Suzanna's tanned hand burned copper beside her etiolated glove.

Lulumae declared and my-my-ed a whole society-wedding train of polite froth saying nothing as she sashayed up the porch steps, raising her fancy skirts so as not to trip. To every stride Suzanna took, she took a half-dozen niminy-piminy steps.

Fingerbone looked at her mistily, like she was either from another planet or the kind of visitation moonshine brings you in the dead of night; she rolled her mottled lips one inside the other, near swallowing the stem of her pipe.

'Ay-ehnd, who is this deah old ch'actah?' cooed Lulumae. 'Good day to you, ma'am.'

Bob and curtsey; Fingerbone rolled her eyes in a fair imitation of senility – or inebriation, which was more like.

'She don't hear too good,' said Suzanna, gruffly. 'Don't talk much and what she does say there ain't a lot of sense in. But I'm sure she knows all that goes on – doncha, Maw?' she hollered in Fingerbone's ear.

The old woman affected palsy and cupped one hand round her ear, followed by a series of lip-smackings. Lulumae's peach-blonde face was frozen in the polite folks' version of horror.

'You want some lemonade, Maw?' hollered Suzanna. 'I

swear to God, ma'am, she's got lemonade for blood. I never knew such a thirst outside of hellfire!'

Lulumae blenched a whiter shade of magnolia. 'Language . . .' she murmured faintly to *mah man*, clutching his arm, as Suzanna strode indoors shouting:

'Grits! Granmaw needs some lemonade! Hotter 'n the devil's armpit out here!'

Lulumae decided she hadn't heard. Suzanna set a fresh glass of liquid at Fingerbone's feet. Pure gin – topped with a few cosmetic strands of lemon.

'Now, folks – goddammit, I'm forgetting my manners, keeping you all standing out here. But you gotta take care of them that has taken care of you. Come on in and get settled.'

NINETEEN

Grits came shuffling through with a tray of coffee, wearing a white starched apron I'd never have suspected her of owning. Lulumae sighed to midair:

'I sure could use th' opportunity to freshen up a little . . .'

'What am I thinking of?' said Suzanna, as if mortified. 'Grits, maybe you could show Miz van Doon to the – washroom.'

'Yiz, ma'am, Miz Comstock,' said Grits and shuffled upstairs, beckoning Lulumae to follow.

'Mr van Doon,' said Suzanna, 'this here's my accountant and business partner, Miz Blanchard. Figured she oughtta be in on this discussion.'

'Pleased to make your acquaintance, ma'am,' said he, and as we shook hands, I flicked through my memory. I knew this man. Van Doon, van Doon . . . I knew the florid face, the iron-grey skullcap of hair, the flashy necktie knotted close enough to choke and skewered with a diamond pin the size of a horse's tooth.

'Been mighty hot, Miz Comstock,' he said, fingering the brim of his hat. 'Ain't the weather for outdoor work.'

'You gotta take it as it comes,' said Suzanna. 'There's always work to do, rain or shine. Only way to get on top of it.'

Darknell van Doon!

Jesus! Don't shit and slurry rise to the top and swill around stinking! Chicago, and van Doon was one of the 'business interests' interested in running me out of town. He was on the board – that collection of respectable-living, well-heeled ruffians behind every rotten racket in the city. And now he was wheeling-dealing out West . . . and had picked himself a Southern belle to marry on the way. What I remembered too was he had an expensive taste in chicana ladies of the night, and there had been a couple of murders and disappearances couldn't be laid on his doorstep. I'd never have seen him settling for a woman fairer than dried straw. The only way he knew how to do was dirty. If *he* was master-minding this cattle syndicate . . . bad stuff.

Lulumae trippety-trapped back downstairs, her pale cheeks now sunset orange, her bloodless lips vampire red. There was a cold gleam in her eyes.

Suzanna poured coffee and lit a cheroot. 'Miz van Doon – Miz Blanchard, my partner and accountant. Seeing's how there's finance to be talked.'

Lulumae's china-doll eyes flickered over me and she turned to *mah man* with a girly pout that looked kind of ridiculous on a woman her age.

'Aw, Darknell – *honey!*' she protested. 'Ah just knew there had to be a reason for mah daddy bringin' his little girl with him! *Ah* sign the cheques. Pleased tuh meet yuh, Miz Blanchard.'

Mah man didn't like that a whole heap. Lulumae sat in triumph and sipped at her coffee, her chit-chat buzzing round the room like a daddy-longlegs, all fragile-seeming

76

and annoying as hell. There was a new cattiness to her, and I watched close for a hint as to what had put the vinegar in the icing sugar. I didn't have long to wait.

'Ay-end, Miz Comstock, when did yew give up the stage? Ah guess a woman has to accept her age, am Ah *right*? Of course Ah don't know a thang about the theatrical world, never having had the pleasure of meeting any *actresses* before. Ah declare, Miz Comstock, y'all must have experienced some fascinatin' – experiences.'

The picture in the bathroom!

Suzanna threw back her head and laughed, which is not what Lulumae had intended. I swear the woman was truly jealous for *mah man*, and saw Suzanna as some kind of threat.

'I haven't been on a stage for fifteen years or more, Miz van Doon. Hell, that was jest a little sideline. More coffee?'

Lulumae managed to put a whole offended flounce into saying that would be most acceptable.

'Waa-aall, Miz Comstock,' said Darknell van Doon, puffed up like a toad in mating season, trying to bluster back some of his authority, 'you appear to have suffered some trouble west of here. I was mightily relieved to find you safe and well. I seen all them signs – I know Injuns, Miz Comstock, and you're in for more trouble, yes ma'am.'

'Well now,' said Suzanna, like a big ship cutting through oily swells, 'we have an arrangement with the Indians. They tolerate us – hell, Mr van Doon, this was their land first. What you seen was the first signs of trouble from No Arms Hackmore. Jest a little warnin', Mr van Doon. A sign of how sweet and accommodating they'd be with cattle. I think you have your answer if you're wise enough to take it. Things'll be fine *so long as it don't go no further*.'

'Darknell done told me all about the dreadful untimely endin' yaw deah helpmate come to, Miz Comstock! Air yew *sure* that was them outlaw ruffians? Sounded like Injuns to me! Yew must tell me more, as one woman to another!' Lulumae burst in over *mah man's* gasping for words. 'And Ah do have such a curiosity about mah fellow human beings!' She placed one hand on Suzanna's arm.

Suzanna tightened her jaw like the hand was a bug she'd be a sight happier swatting. 'A good thing you asked that,' she said, with feigned tragedy in her voice. 'Since I spoke to Mr van Doon here, I have relived that tragic night. I believe if my husband had been less of a man in standing up to their braggin' and bullyin', he might be alive today. But at least he left me a memory I can respect.'

'Oh! Ah have had nightmares Ah was glad to wake from, since Darknell come back from seein' you!' cried Lulumae, snapping a fan out of her bag and banging the air around her flushed face. 'Oh, the injustice! The agony! And Ah'm intooitive about these things, Miz Comstock. Ah'm utterly convinced yew must have blotted out the hideous savage reality! There isn't a white man born could have mutilated a fellow human being! Only an Injun gits that low! They even *eat* the flesh off the corpses while they're still warm! They inflict the most *horrible* deaths! Leastways our boys use a good clean bullet. I don't like to contemplate the details of what those barbaric Injuns do to kill a man. Ah've read *all* the reports in the newspapers. Ah'm of the considered opinion they're the spawn of Satan!'

'Now, Lulumae honey, don't you get yourself all fretted up,' said van Doon, patting her knee.

'Oh, Daddy knows me so well! Ah'm so sensitive it always has been a burden to me. Whah, Ah couldn't even kill a fly. Or a spider even – Ah'm a regular little fuss-budget,' said the steel-cored Lulumae. 'Ey-and, Miz Comstock, however have you managed without a Man to take care of thangs? I jest *depend* on Darknell for most everythang.'

And sign his cheques, I thought, as van Doon's chest threatened to bust the buttons off his shirt.

'Now, sweetheart, me and Miz Comstock got bizniss to

talk,' he said. 'Maybe Miz Blanchard could show yew around, honey.'

'Miz Blanchard stays,' said Suzanna. 'I'll get one of the hands to show y' around, Miz van Doon.'

'Ah do not wish to cause no botheration,' trilled Lulumae as Suzanna hollered into the kitchen:

'Grits! Could you run down and get Lucille or Roo to saddle up a coupla horses so's they can show Miz van Doon around the spread?'

'Right away, Miz Comstock, ma'am,' said Grits, clearly getting one helluva kick out of the act.

'Oh, what an adventure, Ah do declare!' squeaked Lulumae. 'Now, don't let little me hold up yaw bizniss, Darknell – Miz Comstock, Ah'll jest set a while with yaw dear mother. Ah have a way with old people, certainly should with nursing mah dear daddy all through his last illness and all those false alarms.'

Saint Lulumae sashayed out onto the porch. I met Suzanna's eyes. Hoped to God Fingerbone would remain senile and mute – then again, there'd be a heap of fun if she didn't.

TWENTY

'Now comes the serious purpose of our visit, Miz Comstock, Miz Blanchard,' said Darknell van Doon, in Suzanna's office. All at once he was the bull-necked businessman, opening a leather case and pulling out sheaves of paper.

'Seems we have a few problems here in Fortress. Nothing we cain't iron out. Injuns for one: we can get 'em smoked out and that's the end of that one.'

'Waall now,' said Suzanna, 'we seem to have an OK deal with them. Nothing we can't handle as is.'

'But when the cattle come,' said van Doon, 'we cain't

have no war parties and raids. Hell, there's reservations for Injuns now.'

'You do seem to have got yourself fixed on Indians,' said Suzanna wearily. 'You oughtta pay some considerable account to No Arms Hackmore, Mr van Doon. 'Sides which, he ain't alone. Word is we got Cactus Kerensky's boys up there now, and madder en polecats. Jesse James's child jest got his liberty too, Gravedigger James? You must a heard the boy's reputation. Hell, Mr van Doon, you're talkin' about treadin' your way across a snakepit! Least-ways the Indians got land rights, signed and sealed. Way they see it, we're the squatters, and even so there's enough to share. But there ain't enough to go grabbin' yourself great chunks any more. Those days are gone. You gotta turn your mind to desperadoes, Mr van Doon, despera-does so accustomed to the feel of blood on their hands they don't feel right without it.'

'Hail, ma'am, pardon me, leastways they're white men. And they speak a Christian language. You can reason with a white man.'

Suzanna blew a whirlpool of smoke rings and shook her head heavily.

'Miz Comstock,' said van Doon, changing tone and tack to the fruity sincerity of an itinerant preacher, 'you don't need to tolerate sech aggravation. It's no life for a woman, per-ticully one as has been struggling on after the untimely death of her beloved helpmate. No, ma'am, they got reservations now, and them savages as can appreciate an opportunity, why, they'll have schooling and all sorts. They gotta move with the times, Miz Comstock. The old days are done. We got standards and decency and Chris-tianity and it's our dooty to pass this on to these poor heathens.'

Burning down newspaper offices, tenement housing, and rackets the law's paid to turn a blind eye to: those were the Chicago standards of Darknell van Doon. That was his decency and Christianity.

'Share and share alike,' said Suzanna firmly. 'I got no complaints. The man I had was better off dead, tell you the truth, Mr van Doon. But I ain't about to burden you with secrets best buried with the dead. My worry is, what will a bunch of ragamuffin rustlers do when they can pick up a whole herd of dogies at their front door? I'm of the opinion you might do better to find another valley for your syndicate. I been thinking it over, talking it over with my partner here. I can't see you getting the kind of profits you'd be looking for. The valley isn't big enough. And that's my decision.'

'In that case – ' he began, when a shriek ripped through the office door.

'Ah jest *couldn't*! Landsakes! What an idea!'

Suzanna and I leaped to our feet. Whatever the hell had Fingerbone said or done to upset our sensitive guest? But out on the porch, the old woman was only sitting rocking and sucking at the rim of her half-empty glass. Lucille was standing looking puzzled, and Lulumae was wilting against the doorpost like a wax magnolia in the sun.

'Oh, Darknell,' she gasped, 'Ah am flustered! Ah appreciate this is backwoods, honey, but Ah cain't ride that *hawse*!'

Lucille had saddled up Snow, a beautiful bay whose patient eyes held the wisdom of the Sphinx below a bright flash of white that spread over her head and ears.

'Seems a nice animal, darlin',' said van Doon, as puzzled as the rest of us.

'Darknell! Ah never rode a man's saddle in all my days yet! Miz Comstock, you surely have a lady's saddle in yaw establishment?'

'Hell, no,' said Suzanna. 'Don't rightly know what one of them would look like. A saddle is a saddle – ain't it? Lucille?'

Lucille shook her freshly hennaed head. 'A side-saddle, I guess,' she said. 'We ain't got no side-saddle, ma'am.

Ain't never been no call fer one that I can recollect. I tell yuh what, ma'am, I kin lend y' a pair of britches.'

'*Aaaa-oooow*,' wailed Lulumae. 'Ah have never disported mahself in masculine habiliments . . . the ve'eh ahdea is bringin' on one of mah spells!'

'Or,' said Lucille soothingly, 'we got some skirt-bloomers, now I put my mind to it. Yuh recall that Scottish lady rode thru' here when we was jest startin' out, Suzanna? She didn't like th' idea of no britches neither, ma'am, and she'd rigged herself up a costume was more ladylike to her way of seein' it. We got her to leave one behind for interest, I b'lieve.'

'Goddam!' said Suzanna, with a warm laugh. 'Could I forget her? Tales she had to tell – she'd bin to Jaypan, Honolulie, a list of places long as a summer evening.'

'Alone?' gasped Lulumae.

'Ma'am,' said Lucille, 'she was the kind of lady could walk into a cathouse and have 'em sippin' tea and singing "We Will Gather By the River" afore she was through the door. Class, Miz van Doon, like you'd be proud to own as a friend. A'most stuck here, did Miss Isabella Bird, she liked it fine. But a restless sperrit, alwiz requirin' to see whut lay over the next range.'

'It would be a shame if you was to miss out on this fine day, Miz van Doon,' said Suzanna. 'Mebbe if you was to inspect these here skirt-bloomers you might feel soothed.'

'Y'all must consider me foolish,' said Lulumae, mollified. 'Only the ahdea jest took me sideways! Mercy, Ah'd be delighted to ride, Miz Comstock, Darknell has told me so much about yaw valley heah.'

'Let me bring 'em up tuh th' house,' said Lucille.

It took a while, maybe a good half-hour, to get Lulumae into the oddest set of garments I've ever clapped eyes on. There was skirts on top of the bloomers, and the whole thing looked darned cumbersome to me. But Lulumae said it was a most *accommodious* rig-up and we watched them ride down the path. An odder pair it is hard to imagine, the one spare and easy and near silent, the other cushioned and curled and tweetering away with hands fluttering fit to scare the birds off the trees.

TWENTY-ONE

'Yew hev come close to talkin' Ultimatums, Miz Comstock,' said van Doon, once we were back in the office. 'But thangs may not be quite so clear-cut yiz and no as yew would like to present 'em. Comes a question of who has the *rights* on this land, and I got my associates to do a little diggin' theah!'

The boy was beginning to resort to his natural hawg self. The layer of charm was thin and slimy as oil spread on the Mississippi in the wake of one of those pleasure steamers where a person can find themselves facing ruin over the unremarked twist of a marked card. Was no question of 'doing business' with Darknell van Doon, just a question of would Suzanna agree willingly or be forced to it.

'Yii-iz?' said Suzanna LaReine like she was talking to dirt, which she was.

'Now, wheahbouts would yew hev registered yaw land claim, Miz Comstock? I wuz wishin' tuh inspect the legal papers so as I could make yew a fair offer.'

'I don't believe that'll be necessary, van Doon,' I said. 'Miz Comstock and myself have discussed your offer, and we're not interested. You can see how it is in the valley: your stock could not be guaranteed safe pasture, and I have no wish to be involved with any insurance clauses which could bankrupt us both. I didn't inherit a fortune to squander it on a project I consider unsound.'

I was using the *grande dame* tone that had got me past more triple-locked high-society doors than any other newspaper writer in history. It was a trick I'd learned back in New York from the razor-sharp mind of Hal Mayflower-Ames, the most feared and respected man in the business, my first editor. *The higher up they think they are, the more contempt you give 'em, make 'em feel you're doing them a favour, Stanforth! Lah-di-dah the bastards till you got 'em sweating and they'll swear their sainted mother was a Chinese whore so as you'll leave 'em be!*

And Hal had died in his own bed of nothing worse than tireless overwork and a crippled pancreas. Darknell van Doon was the kind he'd have stuffed through a mincer, sold for dogmeat and spent every buck of profit on a jamboree for orphans.

It worked. Van Doon wrenched his necktie loose in the interests of breathing easier. He shuffled papers, searching for the right words and the best way of delivering them. I sat erect. You'd have sworn the blood in my veins was true blue and chill as a dry martini.

'Now then, Miz Blanchard,' he began with the winning whine of a patent-laxative salesman. 'We do hev tew think of tahms changing and changing with the tahms afore they overtake us, yes sirree! Th' days when yew could set up and squat – homestead, pardon me – whatever green pastures took yaw eye, those days are gone, more's the pity. I have always admired independence. I'm a man of honour as always respects an onterprenoor. Known for it. Ask any of my associates and they'll tell you good ole Darknell van Doon is the boy to back an outsider! But when I see the hardship yew good ladies heve to endoor, I ask myself why? *Why?* Th' pioneering spirit is an admirable hooman quality, but these days, Miz Comstock, Miz Blan*chard*, there is no call for suffering. Why, yew two ladies could be swanning out on the West Coast in luxury! There is no need for yew tew be toiling and sweating like men have died for – it ain't right or natural. Yew could be living in refinement as befits yew jest by signing a piece of paper.'

It was a pretty speech as might have touched the heart

of a woman worn out with working the land and gullible besides. But Suzanna LaReine exuded the vitality of a woman who has made hard choices and thrives on them. Me? I hope I appeared as contented as I was, just being around her here in Kimama.

'Mr van Doon,' said Suzanna.

'I do wish you'd call me Darknell, Miz Comstock,' he said with the kind of heartfelt sincerity comes from a man with watered piss trickling in his veins.

'Mr van Doon.' She laid the words down like a sabre blade. 'You seem to be labouring under a misapprehension. I have no wish to sit and fan myself cool on some white balcony in the sun. Everything I have I've worked for. Which makes it mine. My partner here has financed some of my wilder projects. I have no wish to change a thing. Mister, you come here with a proposition: I've thought about it and come up with no. Tell me, how would your backers respond to the notion their investment was at the mercy of the cruel and crawlin' ravages of the worst cut-throats ever fouled the earth?'

'Lawd, Miz Comstock, I already said, th' army kin ketch and try and hang all a them scum plaguin' yaw life and blightin' this bright future faw yew! This here is a law-abidin' civilized country and it's our dooty as citizens to combat any ant-eye-social element we happen upon!'

'My husband thought the same, Mr van Doon. Remind me to show you his grave.'

'But times hev changed, Miz Comstock!'

'From what I understand, Mr van Doon,' I cut in, 'there are a lot more places you could take your proposition and be welcome. The answer is no.'

'Perhaps we should take some refreshment,' said he, scarlet as a crowing cock challenged off the top of its dung heap. 'I will consider ever'thing yew hev laid before me, and come back tew yew.'

'Certainly,' said Suzanna LaReine, every inch a queen. 'Besides, I have to attend to Maw.'

'Waaa-aall, I'll jawn yew presently,' said Darknell van Doon. 'They's a few papers I'd like to peruse.'

'I'll have Grits fetch you some coffee,' said Suzanna, and we adjourned to the porch.

TWENTY-TWO

'How's it goin'?' hissed Fingerbone, raising one ruched eyelid.

'It ain't good,' said Suzanna. 'That hawg-fucker acting like he has an ace in the hole – whutchuh reckon, Typewriter?'

I kept my voice low. 'I know this runt from Chicago. He's part of the outfit got the newspaper offices burnt out. He doesn't know how to piss straight. He's the type to get what he wants by any skuldugging trick you ever had nightmares about. Dealing from a marked pack? The boy was doing that in his baby carriage!'

Suzanna sat by Fingerbone's feet, and the old woman's hands raked around her shoulders like only an old friend can.

'Suzanna, are yuh ready tuh pin back them gorgeous ears and listen tuh this ole sack fulla gin an' piss?'

'Hit me with it, Maloof,' said Suzanna. 'I already been hit with enough today and yesterday to take another slap sweet like a woman's kiss.'

'I cain't string my words together too good, sugar,' said Fingerbone. 'But donchuh worry yuh beautiful haid about this son of a whoremonger. This land is your land, Suzanna.'

'Gawd if you don't talk a mile of bullshit,' said Suzanna wearily. 'Mr Darknell van Doon got all the legal guys sorting that out. Soon enough he'll know my *rights* ain't worth doodley-squat.'

'That's where yuh don't know mother's milk from

moonshine!' wheezed Fingerbone. 'Yuh know I alwiz bin on at yuh let's take a trip tuh Deadwood. Yuh never would, yuh ornery twist-tailed limb a cussedness. Yuh got th' idea – and once yuh got a idea in yuh stubborn head, ain't gunpowder made as'll shift it – yuh got th' idea I wanna raise the ghost uv Janey. Yuh wrong, sweet Sue, yuh wrong like a three-leg possum makin' fancy eyes at a mule. I got reasons for Deadwood, an' I do require a mite of respect afore I tell yuh them reasons.'

'Aw, sheeee-it!' Suzanna dragged out. 'Give you a pitcher of lightning and all I damn hear is Deadwood, Deadwood, like all you hear is the Sacred Heart of Jesus in them cold holy Roman churches! I don't want to hear no dreams riding on still-brewed liquor. Gawd's sake, Maloof, Mother Mary, this is *serious*!'

I knew the old lady had something more to say. Suzanna's bull head had decided it was drinking dreams, but I aimed to find different. Right now, the old woman's jaw was set firm as a trap on a bobcat's tail. Grits came out on the porch.

'Why, ma'am, Miz Comstock,' she said, 'I'd a knocked three times, fell to my knees and curtseyed ef I'd knowed yore highness was out here, pardon my apron. Where are *They*?'

'He's in th' office plotting rack and ruin, the lady wife's out bending Lucille's ear and making a damn fool a that poor horse. Why?'

'Whut time you planning to have 'em eat? I guess we have tuh feed 'em, guess we have tuh give 'em a bed for the night. Me Old China been troublin' me all mornin', requirin' flour and soda and Gawd knows what else, and wouldn't give a word of sense why. Hell, we oughtta jest invite a pack of wild dogs and allee-gators in th' house fer an easy life! Gawd, I hope yuh know whutchuh doin' this time, Suzanna.'

Grits sat on the porch and pulled a bottle from her apron pocket.

'Medicinal,' she said, swigging and passing it over. 'We all lookin' pretty sick.'

'Ef some folks would listen tah the wisdom of the years!' threatened Fingerbone.

'Grits – whatever Me Old China requires, you give it her. She got the damn knowledge about intruders. And Fingerbone, all right, for chrissake, ain't going to be no peace here till you have your say – shoot, y' old buzzard.'

But the office door slammed; smart shoes squeaked across the floorboards; Grits scrambled to her feet; Fingerbone lolled her head and clutched her knitting.

'I'll jawn yew ladies,' said van Doon, jovially. 'I think we can work a way round the problem to ow mootooal advantage.'

TWENTY-THREE

Whatever passel of pizen van Doon had cooked up for us was cut cold by the spectacle of Lulumae and Lucille in the pasture moseying on back home. The sun was spilling deep-gold beams all around us, and by the time Lulumae had re-*freshed* herself, Grits was getting fretful about her banquet getting spoiled, Fingerbone was heaving like a sea of lava, and we still had a final scene to play. The dinner party.

Nary a one of us had realized just what effect a supper like we had together three times a week would have on the hand-reared milk-fed pet-lamb soul of Miz Darknell van Doon, sweet Lulumae, her daddy's darlin' child.

Well, she *lahked* the silver and she *lerved* the china, and she *pahzitively* lit up at the sight of the crystal. You could almost read dollar signs clicking up like a cash register in her baby-blue eyes. The whole crew gradually assembled, clearly togged up for best, and that's when Lulumae commenced to fracture a little. See, none of us had had too much occasion to rub elbows with Southern gentility previous to now.

Outta some east European aristocratic inheritance, Mira Mazole had dug up a black velvet waistcoat sparkling with silver bells for buttons on both sides, over a shot-silk shirt the colour of moonbeams. For the rest she had fancy black rodeo pants cut close to the skin.

Grievous's square face hung over an outfit in tan, studded all over and squeaky-clean: leather turned this way and that; from the fit I guessed this was some dude outfit she'd picked up before her muscles got to relax a little.

Roo wore a white silk shirt all ruffled like a saloon cowboy, and denim the inky blue of new and never been worn before.

Assassina was a vision of scarlet and cerise, a stiletto stabbed through the kind of neckscarf a maharani might have flung around herself for an important international audience. She started almost imperceptibly when she saw Suzanna, and I thought of the murderous stiletto buried an inch into white cotton where Suzanna's neck might have been but for my sixth sense . . . Assassina looked good and sick.

Like a mirage in the desert, Lariat Lucille had decked herself out in shimmering green: a shirt the colour of a grass plain in the sun, her jacket a rainbow of sea and forest, her pants the rich cushioned moss that swathes the rocks of a slow brimming river. Even her dark boots were shot with green stitchery.

Add Grits in a fresh apron homey as apple pie, helping old Fingerbone in like a church usher for her first indoor meal in forty cussed outlaw years . . . Any of this might have been enough to strike Lulumae dumb with her talk of women needing a man to run their lives: the crew clearly needed nothing beyond their own muscle and presence to get by. We were about to sit and drink us a glass of French wine that Suzanna had decided was fitting to her assumed fallen gentility and widowhood, when Me Old China, Rainbow-Wings by the Rushing Waters, elected to join us.

Dressing up was what we all had done: Me Old China had dressed down and painted up. Her sleek copper skin was ablaze with a tapestry of birds, beasts and flowers. In a smock of doe skin pale and liquid as moonlight, her breasts were proud as mountains. A thong of twisted copper and rawhide spilled a dazzling apron of beads and scalloped leather over her metal-muscled thighs. Her naked calves boasted twin paintings of eagles plummeting from knee to ankle, wings rippling as she walked across the floor. Lulumae clutched *mah man's* arm, and gasped: for once she didn't have a tweeting bleating word to utter.

Naturally, we all might have commented. Stuff like: 'Goddam! Me Old China, you sure have gone to town!'

Something about present company made us all hush up, and aside from the shit-kicking glint in Fingerbone's eye, the firework of honed steel in Suzanna's look, there was no sign anything was out of the ordinary.

Grits laid on thick the shuffle and *Would yuh all step inta the dinin' area, ladies an' gent*? We sat around the big table. I heard in fancy society you have to have seating arrangements: man, woman, man, woman, and so forth as if two folks the same sex didn't have a word to say to each other. Darknell van Doon wound up between Suzanna and Mira, facing me. Lulumae got in between Grievous and Lucille, smack opposite Me Old China. Suzanna was at one end of the table, Roo at the other.

Meals we usually ate in the silence of hunger and appreciation. But Lulumae had something to say about every course, words ticking like a praying mantis, her eyes everywhere but on Me Old China, who towered above her even when sitting. Van Doon complimented Suzanna on a table as would do credit in any company. His eyes kept sliding along to Me Old China, bulging like he was being choked.

'How're things with the People?' said Suzanna, solemnly.

Me Old China shrugged, lifted her soup bowl and drained it. 'The old trouble returns,' she said. 'The curse of ash. There is much debate: whether fire will take it away, or water. There is talk of damming the river.'

Suzanna nodded. Van Doon looked nervous; Lulumae gawped, amazed that a savage could string two words together?

'Curse a ash?' said van Doon. 'I din' catch yaw name, Miz – ?'

Me Old China looked straight at him, and said a word I hesitate to reproduce in letters. Something like *Karrwaz-schhmnyebakallawa*. Y' see what I mean? She had chosen this as her name for confusion: the name you give to a stranger you wish to remain unknown to you.

'Yiiii-iiiiz,' said van Doon, clearly out of water like a pike caught ruining the fishing for many a season. 'Waaall, Miz Karrr – em, what is this curse of ash?'

'Blimey,' said Me Old China, 'you ask of things seldom spoken about. My people have been cursed with the blight of ash, and our skin falls like birch bark in the flame of the curse.'

'Disease, huh?' said van Doon. 'Yawl could git that seen to at one of the reservation infirmaries.'

'They turned us away,' said Me Old China, in the hollow voice of tragedy.

Van Doon swallowed and buttoned his foolish lip.

'Don't yaw kind – I mean, Injuns – don't you have herbal remedies?' said Lulumae brightly.

'The plant is not yet sprung to combat the curse,' said Me Old China. 'It is a double curse. While our skin dies, we live. And more children are born than ever before, each one with the blighting mark of the winter.'

This led to a kind of break in the conversation.

'Vesuvius, ma'am,' said Grits with a flourish, placing a huge dish in front of Suzanna, who struck a match on her boot and set it to the white peaks of liquor-drenched eggwhites in front of her. Blue and neon flames played over it and flung her face into a golden silhouette with the strength and power of an ancient statue.

We ate Vesuvius in an uneasy silence, punctuated only by the scraping of spoons and Me Old China's nails on the dishes: she had eaten throughout with her hands, which I guess none of us had ever thought worth noticing before Lulumae's eyes opened wide as the white and naked mouth of a walking catfish. Me Old China then belched loud and long.

'Y' always did enjoy yuh food, huh?' said Grits smoothly, swiping the dishes away from under our noses.

Back in the living room, bourbon and cigars, and Lulumae strapped for a word to say. Just as her eyes lit on the drapes, just the second her coral shark's lips parted, Me Old China leaped to her feet.

'Suzanna – look! It has begun!' she whispered, pointing to her arm. We all leaned forward: there was a long white line from wrist to elbow, twisting like metal under a blowtorch. So that's what she'd needed flour and soda for!

'Gawd!' said Suzanna. 'Does this mean . . .?'

'It's in the blood,' said Me Old China. 'I had better leave you.' Catlike she sprung to her feet and left the room.

'Whut *is* that?' said Lulumae shrilly.

'The curse of ash,' said Suzanna, like she'd been asked what time of day it was. 'She has at most a year to live. Hopefully she'll carry her child to term. But she's a dead 'un.'

The crew shook their heads and bid us good night.

'Miz Comstock,' said Darknell van Doon, after a sombre silence, 'would that be – leprosy?'

'Sure,' said Suzanna. 'A little more bourbon?'

Van Doon's fat face turned a shade to match his wife's dress. 'But – ' he quavered, 'ain't that infectious? In the Bible . . .'

'Waaall, all the tribe call it a curse,' said Suzanna. 'Seems it don't strike unless it's in the blood. And you should see the papooses sprung outta that tribe! It's a double-edged thing, Mr van Doon: you may have a sentence of death hanging over you, but you got fertility like I never seen before.'

I looked to Lulumae to say something, but she had abandoned herself to one of two states: stone dead or in a dead faint.

TWENTY-FOUR

Now it was clear that Lulumae, once revived, was not totally content to spend the night in an Indian leper colony shared with a band of women like she'd never come across nor dreamed of before, even in the lurid tabloids she read. Let alone the foul lusts of No Arms Hackmore and his henchmen! I had a private grin to myself, recalling the sour-mash deadline desperation of hacks I'd worked with, who got their bread and beer money writing garbage like that. The stuff that legends are made of!

However, the alternative being an undefended surrey ride through outlaw territory in pitch darkness, she acquiesced. Suzanna showed *mah man* and herself to their bed, where the mind-blown Southern gentility was a little mollified by clean linen.

Suzanna came and sat in my room. It was the first moment we'd spent alone since the morning, and I acquainted her with the grisly stiletto I'd found in her pillow, clearly meant to transfix her beautiful neck. She set her jaw and lit a cheroot.

'Goddam, Typewriter,' she said, rubbing her brow with a clenched fist, 'I thought van Doon was trouble enough. Seems to me Mercedes finally flipped, or someone else's flipped and wishing to pin it on Mercedes.'

'I go for the first,' I said. 'Assassina's the type got to

leave her signature, Suzanna, she's one killing woman and proud of it. Aside from Angel, who the hell wishes harm to you here?'

'And Angel's been locked up all day,' said Suzanna. 'Shee-it! What Roo said is true: years we've gotten by, more or less good, and all at once we have them two firebrands, plus van Doon on top of the mess.'

Suddenly out of my blank and frantic mind I thought: we are a couple of old broads. Old with no answers, like you bust your cherry so long back you can hardly recall who it was with, you've had your fool heart took and broke more times than the jackpot at a French casino. Old. And Suzanna had taken a mouthful of grade A bile from Angel the day before and had to carry on like nothing had happened out of the ordinary; she'd had to go through a day-long scenario with Poodle-Vomit and Liver-Lips Lulu-mae. I looked at her: she was beat and for the first time almost looked her age. And I wanted to hold this old broad, Suzanna, not like nightingales have suddenly begun to sing, or the moon is dazzling your eyes, but like, hey, honey, I've been there. And a woman needs warmth.

'Now,' said Suzanna, 'whoever it was aiming for my throat and seen me still standing today gotta figure one tiny thing: Suzanna LaReine don't sleep in her own bed nights. Which I always have done till yesterday. Mighty good idea you had, Typewriter. So I figure that if you go for the throat once you'll go on doing it till blood is flowing. Which would be here in your room, Typewriter. So I guess we better sleep in my bed tonight. I'd hate to have your blood on my hands.'

'You want me to sleep in with you?'

Suzanna gave me a long look that started hard, then creased into a sparkle. 'Stick around till I have this mess sorted, Typewriter,' she said and reached out to hold my hand in a warm open-ended grip.

I am a woman who wears her heart on her sleeve and every fool birthday, the evening before I chalk up another year of lost hopes and cussedness, I always sit down and make ice-hard resolutions about how the next year is going to see a change. Then I meet a woman like Suzanna LaReine and I just melt like a river in spring . . . I struggled against a blush and the fireworks her smile lit inside me. We went to her bed, we lay together, and the warmth became heat. All my brain poured out reservoirs of cool and temperate water, while my body welled like the core of a volcano. How do you describe a kiss? And the rest of it? Well, when it matters, you don't. You hold it to yourself like a secret. Suzanna, my golden secret, unexpected, unplanned, undreamed.

And, as I knew only too well, times being what they were, unacknowledged. Come morning, the day would happen to us and there would be no time even for a warm and knowing look. Which I could handle, with the memory of her tender closeness. When she slept, I stayed awake a while, drinking in the moon on the contours of her face, and telling myself not to plan a million dreams, not even to think about tomorrow. Just to sleep in this sanctified hush beside her and be glad I was alive.

TWENTY-FIVE

That was the best resolve. I woke as she was rising: she turned and smiled like the sun on the sea, kissed my brow, and left our bed. Then she paused, looked me in the eyes and jerked her head in my direction. I slid out of bed. She swivelled a picture to reveal a hole in the wall the size of a dinner plate.

'The guest room,' she breathed into my ear. We leaned close to listen. Sure enough: Lulumæ and Darknell and the matutinal conversation of a respectable married couple in good old America.

'Darknell, let's jest get the hail outta here! Whatever

95

yaw plans for development, Ah will not rest easy until Dr LeFevre has tested the both of us and pronounced us clear of infection!'

'Now, honey . . .' said he in a voice of fly-blown syrup.

'Darknell, I'm telling you! That naked savage is diseased! That crazy Comstock woman don't appear to have a natural bone in her body! Why, Ah would not stay here a moment longer! She behaves as if leprosy was nothing worse than a summer cold!'

'Honey, listen to your poppa. We all will git them savages seen by a regular doctor and shipped outta here. There's more than your money riding on this one. With them English backers, darlin', we kin clean up and retire in less than three years. I showed yew the papers, Lulumae.'

'Darknell van Doon, Ah've followed yew through thick and thin and bailed yew out more often than yew'd care to remember. Jest one word of scandal blows this thing apart. Imagine if yaw English lords and ladies get hold of this – '

'Lulumae,' said he, with the sound of greasy lips smacking on a turned-away cheek, 'they's no way on God's earth faw this to git t' England. Why do yew think I chose this valley? Far as the world outside knows, ain't no folks even live here presently. Hell, when last I came and talked tuh that Comstock woman, time I was back home, whut did I say tuh the syndicate? Deserted gold-dust pasture for the taking! Wild country for the taming! You saw the handbills, honey, and you also saw the bank orders falling into the mailbox like leaves in autumn! The army'll run in them godless outlaws, ey – and, hell, if they don't do it, I got contacts'd be glad to raze every stick of them precious woodlands to sawdust! We kin smoke out th' Injuns, and hell, honey, this two-bit outfit a women – ain't a real man born as would take 'em serious.'

More lip-smacking, punctuated by girly giggles and

high-pitched 'Aw, Darknell! Yew know best, Daddy!' Enough to make a good woman puke.

'We better git downstairs, honey,' said van Doon. 'See whut downhome fare Suzanna Comstock calls breakfast and git home.'

'Yes, Darknell.'

Suzanna swivelled the picture back into place and looked at me. We held each other close and strong and went downstairs.

Waall, *damned* iffen we didn't have effusion and gratitude pouring out of our guests like a sewer pipe gushes into the ocean. Suzanna chewed cornbread drenched in syrup and drank cup after cup of coffee while Lulumae toyed with toast and sipped, and van Doon swilled his hog-belly full.

'Waall, Miz Comstock, Miz Blanchard,' he said, dabbing his wet red lips on Suzanna's good linen, 'I have to go back to my board of directors to acquaint them with yaw decision. We all had better set off if we're to reach civilization afore nightfall. Thank yew for yaw hospitality.'

We strolled onto the porch where Fingerbone sat, still in Grits's sprigged muslin, soft-sucking her pipe.

'Ah was so interested tew make yaw acquaintance, Miz Comstock,' purred Lulumae. 'Do pass my little thank-yous to the lady who took the time to show me the spread . . .' And so on.

Van Doon turned to us as Lulumae rustled over to the old lady. His eyes were cold.

'Be sure yew haven't heard the last of this, Miz Comstock,' he said. 'They's more than one way tew skin a possum, yes sir. Yew might find yourself regrettin' yaw decision. Yew have a lot to gain by changing yaw mahnd.'

Suzanna raised one eyebrow. 'Is that so, Mr van Doon?' she said softly. 'If I ain't mistook, sounds like you could be making a threat, don't you think so, Miz Blanchard?'

'Could be,' I said, staring till van Doon looked away.

'Good day to yew,' he snarled, looking over at Lulumae. 'Honey, we have to make tracks.'

The pair of them climbed into the surrey, and were gone.

I suddenly had a clear picture of Lulumae van Doon decked out like a doll in Isabella Bird's bloomers. *They's no way on God's earth faw this tuh git tuh England . . .* ? To my mind this earth belongs neither to God nor man, and I have always ridden outside the laws of both. Suddenly, I knew what to do. I went into the office and hauled out my namesake: the typewriter.

'You busy?' said Suzanna, moments later.

'Gimme a cheroot,' I said, fingers like wildfire on the keys. 'I have an inspiration, Suzanna.'

Suzanna was the kind of woman who could read my mind. I blessed the day I'd stumbled across her unique brilliance. In seconds, I was breathing fragrant smoke and she had set a glass of oak-reared firewater at my elbow. The nectar of the gods and lifeblood to an old hack like me. Time enough later to kiss her gorgeous feet and let her know about my feelings. I had work to do.

Two hours later I was done.

'Suzanna,' I called, 'we have to get these to a mail office. Fast as possible. Can you arrange that thing?'

'Grits been bitching at me about supplies long enough,' said Suzanna. 'Got to be about time to hit town. OK, Typewriter, let's go.' Then she frowned. 'Aw, shit, honey,' she said, 'I gotta sort out this mess with Angel. Aw – double-shit! I'd love to go to town with you and have some fun . . .'

Ended up me and Grievous and Mira saddled up and hit the trail for town, where the surrey full of vipers had ridden only a few hours before. We were in a mood to celebrate, against all the odds. Cuz we had more than leprous Indians and burnt-out pasture going in our favour. We had Lulumae van Doon and her ability to sign cheques or not . . . and we had these letters of mine. Something would bring about the change we wanted.

TWENTY-SIX

'We have to talk,' said Suzanna to the child of her flesh standing across the room from her with hate in her eyes.

'Don't I have to fall on my knees and thank my sainted *mother* for letting me out of a fucking locked shed first?' sneered Angel Star. 'Or perhaps I just oughtta say, *yes ma'am*, and bob a damn curtsey to your every whim like all the fools around here seem to think is natural.'

'I can understand you're fit to bust,' said Suzanna, itching to leather the shit out of her mouthy brat, 'but what the hell else was I to do with Darknell van Doon threatening our whole life? Wise up, kid.'

Angel flung herself into a chair and slouched down all her long length.

'Your life, Suzanna. I only just got here, like your dumb hoods keep reminding me.'

'You could have a life here. What the hell d'you think I brought you out here for?'

'You want an answer? Or you want to just keep talking and be listened to?'

'Yew air one ornery yaller-assed pile of brag and horse-piss!' Mary Maloof Fingerbone swayed in the doorway, waving her empty bottle towards Angel. 'I never have a mother as would own me! Lousy bitch leaves me on a cathouse doorstep in a liquor sack! All my life I dream of havin' a mother – yew got one, yuh gopher turd! Yuh mother's one uh the two finest women I ever meet and th' other one's Calamity Jane. I'd like tuh drown yuh and hang yuh out tuh dry! Wet behind the ears is one thing, soakin' shit atween 'em don't warrant the time to spit at!'

'Well, Suzanna,' said Angel. '*Some*body loves you, after all.'

Now Suzanna had been aiming to be reasonable. Most arguments she'd ever stumbled across or needled up had been resolved with a clean punch or three and a mouthful of cussing. And buckshot, when it was called for. With her own child she felt helpless. Not a comfortable feeling for a strong woman who has piloted her pirate ship alone and then with all its outlaw crew through storms of lead and litigation. Besides she was mightily embarrassed at the memory of her own daughter making eyes at her and grabbing her ass in no uncertain manner. Shit! Life was so all-fired complicated. Suzanna had an ego like the Grand Canyon – breathtakingly fascinating for a spectator, but impossible to fill up. An ego that size thrives a while on flattery, and she had to admit she'd been flattered as hell with Angel's admiration. Angel was the type she went for, from what Mary Maloof had told me – a mean swagger, a tough mouth and a kind of helplessness with it. When Angel's admiration had turned to hatred, Suzanna felt doubly hollow.

'Fingerbone, you're so pissed what's left of your brain's gone fishing and ate the goddam worms. Take your mule-stomped hide outta here! This is family business,' she grated.

'Is *that* yuh family? Suzanna, she cuts out yuh guts and uses 'em for a skippin' rope, else weasels don't suck aigs!' screeched the old lady. 'Why ainchuh kickin' the pissant little fart outta here afore she turns into a goddam dust storm? Or maybe she does that already. 'Pears that way to me, seein' as you got some sorta shit in yuh eye prevents yuh seein' straight. Family! To fuck with *family*!'

'I got my own ways of dealing with things,' said Suzanna. 'And, yeah, this is all that's left of my family and I don't intend to take a mess of rot-brain brown-whisky words to sort it!'

'Liquor's warmer en blood, Suzanna, and I drink

enough with you tuh make us Siamese twins! Where's yuh pride, woman? I tell yuh, Janey's getting the little bitch tap-dancin' on th' end uv her bull-whip from here to Mexico and no way back! Yuh losin' it, Suzanna, yuh losin' yuh steel. I always see yuh strong as a bullwhacker's lash, all butter-cured on the outside and wire-braided rawhide underneath! Yuh actin' like a fried-brain mule got hisself two full bags a feed, an' one of 'em full a bugs – an' *still* he don' know which tuh eat from!'

Fingerbone glared at Suzanna, gobbed at Angel and went lollygagging over to the sideboard. She grabbed a fresh bottle of gut-rot and weaved back to the porch. With the first bite of her favourite snake juice, she mouthed: *Gawd, yuh do nuthin' fuh me all my life: answer an old bitch's prayer! We need Calamity Jane around here, and being as she's dead – let her outta the roastin' pit long enough so she kicks some guts back into Suzanna!*

There was a flash of lightning and a chord struck from the purple clouds of Heaven. Nothing new to Mary Maloof Fingerbone, fact is it provided a good backdrop to the strange animals thronging the porch after a pint or so. But she had prayed. Now what the cock-walloping hell did yuh finish a prayer with? She sucked a half-inch of rotgut in.

'*Answer an old lady's wishes, Lord,*' she muttered, then, 'Aw, fuck it – I wish Janey was here!'

Suzanna bit the end off a cheroot and struck a match on her thigh. As she paced, Angel stared at her like a hooded cobra swaying over something it took for prey.

'I was talking to Typewriter th' other night,' exploded Suzanna.

'I guess she's mighty fine to talk to,' said her daughter, all pack ice and a dash of acid on *talk*.

'Made me think clear,' said Suzanna, stopping in her long tracks and fixing Angel with a laser glare. 'If you don't want to be here, you better make tracks, Angel. Chrissake, this is no jail. I made a mistake. I had this idea you'd fit in. I wanted you here, tell the truth, seeing as I've brought you nothing in your life beyond breathing. Besides, you ain't me. You're halfway your pop.'

'Screw you!' screamed Angel. 'And that's all he did, I bet. What was it – one night? Two? A half-hour down th' alley by a saloon?'

Suzanna cracked her across the face. Well, Angel smiled at that, seeing as it gave her good reason to do what she'd been wanting to do ever since Suzanna'd turned her down and turned out to be her mom. She sprang to her feet and slugged out.

'No good wasting words on you, Suzanna!' she spat.

Fact was, Suzanna could have pinned her down with one hand, eaten a bowl of corn-pone and danced a flamenco at the same time. But she was mightily relieved to be into something she could deal with. She even allowed Angel to land a few punches and faked a bit of a stagger at one of them. She didn't feel right about taking her own child apart. Finally she hoiked one magnificent calf around Angel's knees and flung her flat on her back, sat on her belly and pinned her hands above her head. Angel's flailing legs got slammed to the floor with a quick flick of her thighs. Mother and daughter glared into each other's blazing blue eyes.

'We have to talk,' said Suzanna, flinging one blonde strand of hair from her scarlet face. It was a last desperate try.

Angel spat. 'I don't want to talk to shit like *you*!' she gritted out through clenched teeth.

'OK,' said Suzanna, 'I'll tell you what, and I mean *tell*. You get your dumb ass together and you take your fucking little psycho baby with you. You and Mercedes. I'll give you horses, seeing as that'll shift the pair of you quicker. Besides, and you listen to me good and never forget this, Angel Star. The good you got in you came from me. And some of the bad. But there was no good in your father. The only good I've seen in you is when you're with horses.

That's mine. Ever you want to be around me again, you gotta eat a mile of dirt first. Now get.'

Suzanna stood up, shaking with rage. Angel crawled to her feet and her whole face twisted as she stared at her mother.

'I just want to get a good look at what I never want to see again,' she mouthed and stormed from the house.

'Jesus!' raged Suzanna, on the porch.

Mary Maloof Fingerbone opened one eye. What a friend we have in Jesus! she thought.

'Yuh better see 'em off,' she said. 'Trash don't move without yuh boot it real hard.'

Suzanna kicked the porch post so hard the house shook. 'I'm gonna get stinking!' she declared.

'That's mah girl!' said Fingerbone, passing the bottle.

TWENTY-SEVEN

'I swear I tied on a load last night, by God!' The woman stretched and her knuckles cracked hard against solid wood. 'Sheeeee-it! I feel like I slept a hundred years! Whar's the goddam light in this place?'

She sat up stiffly and cracked her head.

'Is this some kinda fuckin' joke?' she roared. 'When I get my hands on the son of a bitch put me here, I'll get him dancing a tango on the end of my whip or my name ain't . . .'

Her voice boomed back at her out of the darkness. She'd been in some tight spots and tight as a raccoon's asshole most spots she'd been in, but – jiminy! – this was new.

'Can't sit up, can't stretch out, can't see a dadblamed blink of daylight,' she grumbled. 'My damn head feels like I musta spent the night on a bender and slept on a rail!'

She thumped her considerable fists on the wood over her head.

'A joke's a joke, yuh dingleberries! C'mon, fellas, lemme outta here!'

But there was only a silence so solid she felt it fold around her like slow cold water oozing along her body and up her neck. All she could hear was her own breathing. And the quality of darkness was like she'd never known: darker than a starless night or a shuttered room when a candle has died. It was like stepping into the night from a bright saloon, until your eyes got accustomed – but this darkness didn't change.

'I been struck blind!' she said, reaching one hand up to her face to check, were her eyelids open. They were, and she barked her elbow painfully against the low wooden roof. Folk had said once her cussing mouth made blue sparks and right now she wished to hell it was true.

Where the blazes was she? She moved one leg slightly, and thwacked up against more wood. The other leg was the same.

She had never been the type to sit and wait for apples to fall out of the trees. Found it damn near impossible to wait for daybreak or nightfall. OK! If some ratfuckers had foozled and bamboozled her into whatever stinking kettle of kerfuffle it was she was in right now – her only interest was how to get out and get her own back! She'd sweated shit for her reputation and wasn't no one going to brag they'd bested *her*.

She groaned as she wriggled her arm to push at the wood over her head. They musta watered the moonshine with lightning: every muscle ached like poison. Some lousy sense of humour! Sides, today she was setting out West again, with Mary Maloof, try to find some new hell for her itchy feet to kick around. *She had things to do!* She braced her body against the floor and shoved, only to fall back sweating after nothing but a creak and a hand dug full of splinters. The pain made her see red, red tore the ache out of her muscles, and she heaved as hard as she'd had to more than once when a wagon wheel was buried in a slurry of mud, and god-damn-it-she'd-always-gotten-the-bastard-wheels – *OUT* – !

'So what the blazin' shit is holdin' this down?' she bellowed.

She lay breathing deep gasps in the eerie silence and fetid eclipse of *wherever* the goddam hell she was! Now she could smell her own sweat and with it came a rancid stink enough to make a mule gag its guts out.

'Locked in with a lousy polecat!' she raged, and thundered her fists over her head regardless of pain or caution. She had fists like sledgehammers and there were busted jaws and ribs all over who knew the truth of *that*! After this little escapade, there'd be a heap more, she promised herself, as blood rushed through her head in a meteor storm of stars.

And suddenly the wood splintered! The sound spurred her on, and her legs lashed up in one of those throat-chops she'd always admired and learned from her outlaw sister.

'Yay!' she hollered as the wood shredded and tore.

Freedom!

But something flooded through the gaps she had made, cold and heavy like buckshot, pouring into her face and eyes. Still there was no light and she rocketed upwards, clawing and scrambling, kicking her way . . .

'Fer chrissake!'

She looked around. Night. Stars. Sky. Air.

Now she could see where she was.

All around her in the gloom were – crosses? Angels?

'What the fuck is going on?' roared Martha Jane Canary Dorsett Somers King Hickok Hunt Steers Dalton Wilson Washburn Combs Buck Burke – Calamity Jane! Spitting out earth she hauled herself out of the grave.

TWENTY-EIGHT

Rainbow-Wings by the Rushing Waters had not closed her eyes all night. Sleep had been replaced by an open-eyed trance, where she worked with the forces of night to bring some kind of resolution to all the shattered shards of the day.

Suzanna. Usually a kingfisher beam of light played from her body, with flashes of scarlet and vermilion when she laughed and loved and brawled and hustled her happiness. But today, there had been little spark from Suzanna. She had thrown up a shield against the two from the West and their world ways. Dead from the neck down, man and wife linked only by a love of paper money and power. And the scene with Angel the night before had done a deal to dampen the mountain-ash flame of strength and sureness burning in Suzanna LaReine.

'I knew Angel was trouble,' said Rainbow-Wings by the Rushing Waters, 'but I knew as well that she had to be here, for flesh and blood calls to its own through the years.'

She sat back on her heels, rubbing the body paintings away. They had been her protection for the time she ate with the dead ones, but now she needed to be in touch with all the elements.

Sure, the dead ones had been shocked by the inspired fake of the curse of ash, but she had also seen the pictures in the sluggish mind swirls of the man: her people, reduced to a paupered mass, marching south under armed escort. And every person in his mind had the same face, a hook-nosed shifty-eyed savage. That was his wish for her and all her people.

When it came to Suzanna and her crew – those women who had loved and delighted her – his pictures were less clear. They would be made to leave Kimama, of that he was sure, but Darknell van Doon had a lot more thought-wishes for them. She had watched him talk to Suzanna, and seen a bland blonde doll in his mind; only the face was similar enough to be recognizable. The doll was partly clothed and spread on a bed with a come-hither pout aimed at Darknell van Doon. It was the same with all the other women: he had the idea that, given scanty silk and lace underwear, each would want to have his body close to theirs.

Rainbow-Wings by the Rushing Waters frowned. Surely it was clear that none of these women wanted him within a thousand miles. The man was blind, she decided, blind to anything other than his own wishes.

It was different with Grievous – when he spoke to her, his mind threw up a picture of her standing over him with a whip. Her face was a grotesque parody of doll-like power. His thoughts were different too with the new woman, Typewriter, fondly, remembered Fools Rush In. His image of her was one of death: by drowning, by bullet, by rope. He had a whole whirl of images about her, centred on fear and fire.

Typewriter. Fools Rush In. The Indian woman smiled, savouring the ceremony they had enjoyed together. That woman walked in swirls of indigo, and now Suzanna's feet were haloed by a violet mist. A good union, she thought, and wished it well.

But the deadhead dollar-slaves were determined. The word *robot* came into her thoughts. Not a word she knew, but that was nothing to be surprised about. Words and pictures came to her from languages she would never know, civilizations undreamed of, cultures long since dead. And now, the earth and air reminded her, she should be welcoming the butterflies. It was time. She shuddered, all at once filled with a sense of the fragility of their wings. There had been a metallic quality to the nightmare visions of Darknell van Doon and she buried her head, seeing a million fabulous wings shatter like glass against steel.

She conjured the proud condor, and its feathers and bones exploded with buckshot.

Still the thought of wings stayed with her. This was a threat to be hoaxed and hexed with air. Flames swept through a forest in her mind, so fire was needed too. And then came to her vision a great flood, and with it mountains surging upwards from a plain. Her mind cleared. Air, fire, water, earth: if Kimama was to be saved, all the elements would have to be called together.

Rainbow-Wings by the Rushing Waters rolled a smoke. Through the blue haze, the hologram of butterflies returned, and she scried a flying thing that would be made of something she had never known, something strong enough to cut sheer through the fool's-gold of Darknell van Doon and his nightmare plans.

TWENTY-NINE

Vega.

Vega?

Vega!

The finest of all the machines she had taken up solo. The record-breaking flight across the Atlantic had been a white-winged gift in *Vega*. She had become one with the plane, their destinies interlinked, so that when death by drowning had stared her in the face, she didn't care. Because it wasn't just her any more . . . she had metamorphosed into a fine-tuned instrument, part steel, part flesh.

Vega . . . when you wish on a star . . .

What was it doing here . . . who had restored it to pristine beauty? She marvelled at its proud clean lines and tried to get her bearings.

She felt like the first human being on earth. There were

no tracks behind the plane wheels in the short thick grass: it was as if some giant had simply placed it there like a child playing with a toy. She had not been in this valley before: the craggy heights above her held no familiar landmarks. The nose of the plane pointed up the valley, this long low scoop of spring-green turf. She liked it very much, the valley, the plane, the freshness of the day; every step brought a feeling of elation, but she had a nagging doubt that she had left something very important unfinished. But what?

She sat in the plane's shadow and lit a cigarette. Think clear, she told herself, three hours of thought is better than jump in and rush and crash. Let 'em wait! She smiled, remembering the tanned leanness of Neta Snook, her first instructor, and her sparse words of wisdom barked out through lips ever-weaving smoke and smiles.

Suddenly, she gasped with pain as her own voice rang in her head:

We are running north and south!

She was in a cold sweat of terror.

We are running north and south!

Where did that come from? And why the overwhelming fear? She had nerves of steel wire-drawn like the frame of the magnificent machine behind her. She had faced death many times, and these nerves had arced her across the Lethean waters like lianas swinging over an Amazonian river. And even with the thrill of terror in those echoing words: *We are running north and south!* – even with the terror she felt a sublime certainty of calm, as if she would never be frightened again.

She stood up and stretched in this first day of spring warmth and light. There was somewhere she had to go, something she had to do. She frowned momentarily; her mind drew a blank. She swung into the cockpit, and looked at the compass. As she did so, the needles swung and settled: due west. Then back. Back and forth like a pendulum hexed to madness.

'Wondered when you'd get here, kid!'

'Neta!' she gasped. 'But didn't you . . .'

The tall lean woman beside her stretched and yawned. 'Hell knows what I did and didn't do, kid. I been hanging round like a loose limb for an age. Couldn't do a damn thing till you got here.'

'Was it you fixed up *Vega*?'

'Nope. Just came over that hill there a while back, and she's sitting here, pretty as a virgin on a first date. That's when I knew you'd be along some time. What gives, kid?'

'Well, damned if I know, Neta.'

'Seems like we're to go due west. Take her up, kid. I guess *you* know how.' Neta Snook grinned that lazy oh-shucks grin, just like she had years before when she'd had to admit, *Kid, you know all I know – now get up there and knock their eyes out staring at you!*

For the first time, Amelia Earhardt started the engine and took off with no clear idea of where she was going and why, and not a trace of worry about either. Whoever had resurrected *Vega* and fixed the compass that way knew what they were doing. Maybe it was a publicity stunt: *American Heroine of the Air Flies Blind and Dazzles Spectators*. Time would tell.

They cruised westwards over the sparkling peaks.

THIRTY

'So what's the deal, Typewriter?' said Grievous, as we neared the western pass. 'Don't gimme that *got-tuh-git-supplies* horseshit Suzanna give me – she don't pay no never-mind tuh Grits bitchin' and moanin'.'

'Yeah, come on, Typewriter,' said Mira, rolling her eyes. 'You and Suzanna got something cooking up between you?'

God, I hoped so! But I kept my voice even. I ought to

know better than spend a night with a woman like Suzanna and be in love when I wake up.

'Yeah!' said Grievous. 'I heard yuh machine, that type-writer thang yuh wuz named for, goin' clickety-clack all damn mornin'. Whose name yuh got in yuh sights now?'

It was easier to talk along that line than answer the questions floating around in Mira's eyes; questions that reflected the delighted turmoil in my heart.

'I reckon we can stir up a hornet's nest for van Doon – '

'I'm gonna lace his hide with lead!' raged Grievous.

'Uh-oh, Grievous. That's not my way. I reckon the only way to stop him is to cut him, but deep, right where it hurts: with him, that's straight in the wallet. He can't do a thing without folk to invest their money. Right? He can't advertise over here being as he's used up his credit all over the States. He's going for English speculators. I'm gonna get his name hung high across every newspaper in England and no one'll be fool enough to trust him with a red cent.'

'Sounds OK,' said Mira.

'It's the best I could come up with,' I said, shrugging. 'All my life I've been amazed by how twitchy folks get at the printed word. You can tell 'em talking till you're blue in the face; put it on paper and it's like throwing a firecracker in a saloon: some fool yells "Dynamite!" and everybody starts jumping out the windows.'

'I'd still like to beat the shit outta that spitball,' said Grievous. 'Whassa matter with this van Doon? He didn't take no for an answer?'

'You got the bastard in one,' I said.

Swallering Gulch, the nearest excuse for a town, was a good day's ride sunup to sundown. There was little there now, Grievous said, beyond a run-down general store a tumbleweed hobo wouldn't bother to piss on, and two or three saloons ready to mop up the skimpy wages of all the hands for miles around.

'Used to be called Golden Gulch back in the olden days,'

she said, as we headed through the pass, 'on account of yuh could go wadin' in any stream thereabouts and walk out with yer boots plated solid gold.'

'What happened to the gold? They clean it out?'

'*Clean* it out, sugar? It got flooded out. Some big-shot land shark bought the claim to a wedge of land clear above all the others. He built hisself a errigation system, diverted every trickle of water his way, so's he could pan out the best first. Th' ole boys din' like that a whole heap, so they put dynamite tuh all the pipes he'd laid. The whole of Main Street was awash and folks usin' boats fishin' for nuggets. Straight after that come a twister tuh finish it all off, and by th' time the place was dried out, all the gold was gone, swallered up!'

'Even now, when the rains come, folk get frisky,' said Mira, chuckling. 'Whole bits of road just turn into a quicksand – was a wagon and team of four swallered entirely four–five years back. So they call it Swallering Gulch. Swallered a mile of hopes and dreams, and plenty more to get swallered yet.'

The country we were riding through was just a touch greener than desert, with rocks ridged like dead trees sitting around, and trees dry as rocks stuck up here and there.

'Time was you could find a little fun in Swallering Gulch,' said Grievous ruefully. 'Clean out them *pro-spectors* at poker, and so much gold around was no hard feelin's.'

'I give it ten, twenty years and they'll be no town at all,' said Mira. 'Used to be they had rodeos and carnivals – you recall that, Grievous?'

'Yup. And dancing. Hell, we even seen a the-*ay*ter play come through once. On'y then folks got a mite too inter-ested in where we come from . . . so we steered clear.'

We stopped by a little slab of water lying near the path. The horses drank deep and we soaked our heads against the noonday sun. I could see what looked like fragments of a broken mirror scattered clear across the luckless landscape; we saddled up and picked our way from one to the next alongisde a sandy ooze Mira said grew to a river when the seasons gave it heart enough to swell a little before freezing.

The first dirt farm shimmered into sight. Well, the buildings of a farm, standing like tombstones after a plague. No one had lived here in a long time, to look at the cracked window frames, sagging splinters of an old corral fence, a pump black with rust.

'The good earth's just got lifted off hereabouts,' said Grievous quietly. 'Ain't the strongest rooster on this earth could raise a crow at what yuh'd scratch outta this land.'

We set off at a brisk trot and found us some rooms with no problems at all, just a dusty sigh of wonder that folk would want to spend a night in Swallering Gulch. Then we hit the mail office cum general store and I sent my letters. Grievous stopped as we were leaving and pointed out a poster of two smiling women.

'I know them two,' she said excitedly. 'Whassit say?'

I told her and she slapped one mighty fist against her palm.

'Damned if it ain't a good sign, Typewriter. *I* cain't see a way outta this mess without there's some blood shed and bones broke. Shit! Looks like we might have some good entertainment this evenin' after all. Whoooo! Just might be the answer to my prayers!'

I looked at the poster again. Maybe Grievous was right. But I pinned my hopes on the letters I'd just sent out like doves, making a wish they'd come home to roost with something a hell of a sight more powerful than an olive branch in their beaks.

THIRTY-ONE

Edinburgh, Scotland, August 18—
How her bones ached! Every one of them nagged at her
with every movement: *You are middle-aged and it is high time
you settled down, Isabella!* The pains even woke her in the
night, when dreams had taken her back to the Rockies. At
the precise moment when the shadowy figure on the horse
ahead turned and she would see again *his* glorious face,
mortal pain jabbed her to consciousness and she would
wake in the chill of three o'clock of an Edinburgh morning,
when nothing is well, and she moaned at the needle-sharp
ache in every limb. In the Rockies she had ridden all day
and never had a twinge; she had slept on bare ground
beneath ice-white stars and never woken other than wide-
eyed with wonder at the bright new day! Her soul yearned
for the purple-misted heights where she would shiver
awake as she drank coffee in a tin mug and be uplifted by
the rosy-fingered dawn in this delightful Eden. *He* would
always push her to ride on to a camp place at dusk long
after she was weary, so that the next day would show a
new vista of delight to share with him.

But here in the granite city, she only knew the sun had
risen when the slice of sky between square buildings
became a dull recognizable grey rather than clouded starless darkness; it was day when the mist clung like damp
cotton wool rather than hanging in the sick-green cloying
tatters of night. Early evening, and the chill drove her back
to toast and gas-lit comfort, evenings of bridge and war-
bling recitals . . .

Isabella! she warned herself as tears rose unchecked.
But only yesterday evening, Gracie McKinney had been
singing 'Ae Fond Kiss'. She had always thrilled to Rabbie

114

Burns, and her throat had constricted as Gracie sang –
surely deaf to those timeless words!

> Had we ne'er lu'ed sae blindly,
> Had we ne'er lu'ed sae kindly,
> Never met and never parted
> We wa'd ne'er be broken-hearted . . .

To sip milky tea and nibble at dry scones after such a
song! Sacrilege to her memory: neither Rabbie Burns nor
Rocky Mountain Jim would have stomached such pap!
While she had never held with liquor, at 40,000 feet above
sea level nothing else would warm a body through at
night. Damn Gracie McKinney and her sweet voice! Oh to
forget, to forget!

And where the New World had always accorded her an
instinctive courtesy, even in the roughest saloon, she was
regarded with an embarrassed curiosity in her native land.
A veiled interest which said little to her face and buzzed
with snide speculation behind her back. What had it
mattered in the plains and mountains of America that she
had chosen to live her life unmarried and boldly travel
alone? It had merely inspired all her guests and guides to
outdo each other in hospitality and chivalry.

Ah! Chivalry! Isabella drew the chill sheets up around
her neck. Only yesterday another of the sepulchraves had
left his card. One of the band of widowers who 'paid calls'
on unmarried ladies of a certain age, and who, if not
discouraged, would make a habit of calling regularly. After
a discreet and passionless interlude of tea and conversation as dry as a water biscuit, there would be murmured
talk of a mutually advantageous arrangement, for: *Does
one not, at a certain age, Miss Bird, begin to wish for companion-
ship? We grow no younger! We cannot cheat the Auld Enemy!*

But she *had* grown younger! Every breath of mountain
air, every scent of sumac and pine, the sound and sight of
torrents white as wild ermine roaring through the trees:

all had brought impassioned youth racing through her blood again. She had never written so well as when she wrote of America! And had *he* not died – who's to say what would have happened? She stilled her welling heart, and steeled herself to rise in the chill room, grimacing at the touch of her practical woollen gown and the felt slippers which spoke of middle age and decrepitude in a cold climate. She was determined not to grow old on this soil, but the last three times she had set out resolved to book her passage back to life, a sudden panic had filled her. The whole world ahead of her – and no matter where she went, a pair of grey eyes she would never see again on any continent, a noble brow lost to eternity but for her humble tribute in prose. With little hope she went down for the post.

What she found in the sepia gloom of the hall set her heart racing. A letter postmarked some four weeks earlier from – America! Could it be . . . ? She berated herself for a sentimental fool. She had seen him buried, after all, and played through her mind every way the sparse inscription over his bones might not be true. She recognized neither the handwriting nor the name on the postmark. The letter burned a hole in her pocket until she had set the tea tray and climbed back into bed. She added a whole teaspoon of sugar rather than her usual half. Perhaps that was what brought the flush to her cheeks as she turned the sealed envelope over and over, as if by handling it she could divine its contents.

She opened it with her thumbnail. Set her eyeglasses on her nose and unfolded the sheets of close-typed paper.

Kimama, July.

Dear Miss Bird,
You may well not remember me, but I met you a good while ago in Chicago, where the newspaper I was working on had the good fortune to publish your series of travel articles, 'A Bird's-Eye View'. I am Helena Stanforth, who had the privilege of signing you up before that arson attack.

I am writing from Kimama, which you may remember as Fortress, where Suzanna LaReine and her outfit have very fond memories of you. You came into our minds recently when we had occasion to use one of your riding habits.

Now, if you do remember me, you will recall the reputation I had as a woman who didn't say good morning without there being a story to be had behind it. Folk don't change! I am sure that you are still gazing eagerly over the next horizon and delighting all your readers with your unique way of bringing places to life on paper. I am writing to ask you a tremendous favour. As always with me, the answer can be yes or no and no hard feelings.

You must recall Kimama – Fortress – heaven on earth for Suzanna LaReine and her crew. Plenty of land for horses and crops. Now there's a syndicate trying to muscle in here and use the land for cattle. They are using the money of English investors who will never see hide nor hair of a steer, nor realize the danger to their investment.

This valley is a godsend to lawless bandits and ruffians who abuse its beautiful thick forests and caves with their ruthless presence. So far, they keep their distance from Suzanna LaReine, choosing to inflict their wanton natures miles away. But introducing cattle will cause bloodshed. We both know that justice has a way of catching up with you and their time will come.

I was not at liberty to reveal to you how the Chicago newspaper offices got burned down, being in fear of my own life for some good time after, but I can now say that the same apology for a man that masterminded that is behind this scheme. Darknell van Doon. You may have seen newspaper advertisements for investment in England: there will be a mention of huge profits on cattle raised in the newly opened West. This spells death to one of the last unspoiled valleys out West, as well as no security on the investment. Darknell van Doon is an oil-tongued reptile pirate in a fancy suit.

Knowing your love of America and freedom and beauty, I am asking you to make it known in England that this advertisement spells financial ruin to any investors as well as destroying the livelihood of a good outfit. I would also like to extend a warm invitation to you to come and visit with us here as soon as you can – we would all be delighted to get reacquainted with you after all this time.

　　With best wishes,
　　Helena Stanforth

Suddenly, the room was warm again – almost. She drained her cup and dressed, with a set to her jaw that would have sent the sepulchraves bleating into their tartan mufflers.

By noon, Miss Isabella Bird had posted a half-dozen letters to Fleet Street, thrown a few essentials into her portmanteau, and was headed for the train station, with a one-way ticket to the West Coast of America in her handbag.

Life, she thought, drawing her skirts around her in the steamy dim carriage, is what happens when you're lost for any other plans.

THIRTY-TWO

Something heaved in the primeval ooze. A great two-humped shape struggled just below the surface and thick bubbles broke through the surging wallow. A limb flailed and sank again in the cloying morass. A rounded lump pushed upwards, plastered with strands of what might have been vegetation: it was as if the world was just beginning, and primitive life was being moulded from the oleaginous quagmire.

Two massive shapes heaved upright and stood like crude clay prototypes of the human form, leaning against each other at the shoulder. Lips parted under the mire masks and showed teeth and mouths of brilliant white and pink against the dark dripping masks.

'*Yowza!*' threatened one mouth.

'*Urrrgh!*' groaned the other.

Pow! One mighty fist slugged into a mudcapped shoulder, feet wheeled as if on a downhill racer and *THWAP!* a mighty body splattered into the ocean of mire.

'Zapped!' A stick of a man in emcee tails skipped over a tongue of mud flying his way. *'HeeYA – aaAND, aWAN, aTWO, aTHREE, aFOUR, a – FIVE . . . NO, FOLKS! THIS IS ONE GIRL THEY CAN'T KEEP DOWN, WRASSLIN' ROWENA IS ON HER FEEEEEEEET!'*

Wrassling Rowena was up again! Yes, folks! Can a body take this kind of punishment? Sure she can, while there's folk fool enough to pay good money to watch her. Tiger-Tooth Terry, her opponent, flexed gobs of mud from her colossal arms and swung out like a pile-driver . . . the bell ding-a-linged in midswing! Wrassling Rowena twisted her hand and yanked Terry full length to slide hard and fetch up against the cornerpost to shake the ropes so they twanged the emcee to the floor like a stone from a catapult. The crowd roared. They loved this, never tired of seeing it, always looked like an accident.

But each of the fifteen rounds they fought was as carefully rehearsed as any pas de deux Nijinsky had ever executed on a Paris stage, and the audience in Swallering Gulch showed a damn sight more appreciation than kid-gloved clapping and the silken flapping of fans.

Tiger-Tooth Terry poured a gallon of water over her head and spat a fountain of mud. Wrassling Rowena did the same. They exchanged a wink through streaming masks. Five rounds to go and they could quit for the night and get some serious drinking started. In the ring they were enemies, outside, they were the terrible twins. Rowena had fought her way into this world thirty seconds ahead of Terry and they'd been slugging it out ever since, egged on by their loving momma, who was only sorry she'd been born too late to earn a living busting heads and asses. It was what she did best, after all, and she taught her girls everything she knew. The girls did her proud.

But she had passed on, and twelve good folks and true

had been required to carry her sumptuous coffin to its resting place. The twins carried on her memory, coast to coast.

We met them back in Helga Klapperz, the brassiest brightest brawlingest bar in the town. They were wonderfully clean with pink shiny faces and identical manes of tawny hair. Their shirts were plastered with embroidery, only instead of flowers, they had a pattern of clenched fists and arms with bulging muscles. Grievous had come across them in one of her many stretches – they'd been given a token sentence for busting heads outside the ring – and the three had shot together like limpets on a rock. All three were big-built and packed with muscle, but the twins had a wide-eyed baby's view of the world. Grievous had a nose for bad company and lowlife and a conscience besides. They had asked her to join them once she was out. She thought she must remind them of their dear mom. She was toying with the idea when Suzanna strolled into her cell one day and bust the pair of them out two weeks later. The twins went legit and got famous: papers and posters everywhere, and Grievous figured she'd be best to keep a low profile. Besides, she'd found Suzanna, a soulmate as far as law-abiding went.

'Yowza, Grievous!' said Rowena – could have been Terry – and thumped her shoulder.

'Yay, Grievous!' said Terry – could have been Rowena.

'Now whichuh yuh all-fired bobcats is which? Lemme see yuh teeth.'

Twin faces split into twin grins.

'Erri old oof ong uh eff,' said one.

'Eena old oof ong uh ike,' said the other.

'Terry got a gold cap on the left side uh her mouth, Rowena's is right. 'S the only difference between 'em,' said Grievous. 'Meet mah friend, Typewriter, mah friend Mira – Terry and Rowena.'

'So where have you been, you old sinner, uh?'

'I ben busy,' said Grievous.

'Where you living, Grievous?'

'Aw, east aways,' said she vaguely. 'Nice spread. You?'

'Well now,' said one twin, 'we're still on the road. Getting mighty tired of it. Maw always said to quit when you're ahead and we're still ahead so we ain't quit yet.'

'Been thinking about it,' said the other twin. 'We got enough money, jest couldn't figure out what we'd do if we stopped wrassling.'

'Uh-huh,' said Grievous, carefully.

Mira and me went to get more drinks.

'What do you think of the girls?' she said.

'Pretty powerful stuff.'

'I think Grievous is itchy for them to come to Kimama and join us till the trouble's over, and maybe beyond.'

'What do *you* think?'

'I think we could use muscle, and even if we don't, it's kind of reassuring to have around the place. I know Grievous'd be a lot happier.'

'What about Suzanna?'

'Figure you'd know more than me about Suzanna,' said Mira with a wicked smile. 'You have Suzanna's *ear*, at the very least. Nah, anything Grievous does is fine with Suzanna.'

As we took the bottles back to the table she murmured, 'I've never seen a typewriter blush before. It's a fine sight. But I'm just warning you, Typewriter, don't fall in love too fast. You're a good woman. Jesus, who am I to dish out advice? Don't fall in love *first*.'

Now what in the hell did she mean about that? What did she know about Suzanna that I didn't? I put her words on ice and got down to the serious business of bourbon and conversation bawled over a honky-tonk piano and some European woman with a smoky growling voice singing the kind of songs my foolish heart laps up like cream.

THIRTY-THREE

The morning found Terry and Rowena riding with us, chirpy as folks on vacation. The next little while in Kimama would be no picnic, but a dozen skunks couldn't have turned those gals' twin noses from the trail of a real big fight.

Two distant figures shimmered out of the dust trail ahead of us. We stiffened a little. The only place they could have come from was Kimama – what had happened? Close to, the pair turned out to be Mercedes and Angel, who sat straighter, slouching their jaws lower as they saw us, swaggering from the waist up – about as much as a body can do by way of bragging on horseback.

'Trouble,' said Mira.

'Holy shit,' said Grievous.

I recalled the stiletto piercing Suzanna's pillow and found my body setting hard as cooling steel.

'Goin' somewhere?' said Mira.

'Your queen's told us to git,' said Assassina, like she was the wronged party. 'Thrown her own child to the mercy of the four winds.'

'Don't explain you, Mercedes,' said Grievous.

'We were both told to pack and get,' said the murderous scarlet mouth.

'We've always done what we're told,' said Angel, a pale smirking shadow of Mercedes's pure venom. I had a flash of pity for the kid. Because she was Suzanna's kid? Maybe. Or just because I'd thrown myself out of home about her age, and I knew how tough it could be. And I was raised with more guts than Angel Star'd ever grow into.

Mercedes snarled, 'You think you're safe in Fortress? Suzanna's loco, Grievous. Who's she going to jump on to next?'

'Or off of?' spat Angel, glaring at me.

'Maybe she doesn't feel too good at the idea of a blade in her neck,' I said to Mercedes who flinched from looking directly at me.

'You want to change words with yellow-tongue wolves?' said Mira to all of us. We started moving ahead. Only Angel got the fool idea to boot Rowena's horse in passing by way of au revoir. She never should have done that.

Rowena danced her horse around. 'I never witnessed dogshit ridin' a horse before,' she said, real low and slow, 'leave alone dogshit poured into boots raisin' itself to kick another person's horse.'

'Yeah?' said Angel, proud and kinda delighted, firing herself up to the fight ahead.

'Yeah,' said Rowena, taking the opportunity to clean her mouth out across Angel's path. 'Yeah. Course I've had occasion to step in all kinds of shit from time to time. Leaves a stink on yuh boots. I've even drove through it, besides, and got me an all-fired mess on the wheels.'

'Most times I've seen a barrel of hawg-grease, it's getting rubbed into something to make it slippery, or getting fried,' said Angel Star. 'Never heard a tub of hawg-grease try to talk before.'

'Seems like dogshit's damn ignorant and blind with it,' said Rowena, to midair.

'Seems like hawg-grease borrowed itself a jackass's brain and getting ideas,' said Angel.

'There's two places for dogshit,' said Rowena. 'And one of them's lying flat on the ground.'

She set her face in a way that said the introductions were good and over. She passed the reins to Terry, sitting poised like a massive shadow, and sprung to the ground. I watched Angel's face. The murdering bitch had the grace to look a little troubled: on horseback, Rowena's bulk might have been taken for a woman run to fat; on the ground she stood neat on her feet, every muscle taut and waiting to hammer something to hell. And Angel was so fired up to prove herself to her new buddy, she just leaped to the ground and threw the reins at Mercedes.

The pair circled each other slowly in the dust, Angel sinuous as a glittering snake striking at glass in a sideshow; Rowena powerful as an ox. Angel was the first to lash out one tight fist, straight at Rowena's midriff. The punch landed nowhere as the big woman flew back a pace, throwing Angel off balance and sprawling from a contemptuous little flick of her wrist.

Angel staggered upright and dived back: she had the sense to know a clinch would crush the breath out of her.

Rowena ploughed forward as Angel's arm darted out again, caught the wrist in a mighty fist and flipped her on her back with a crack like firewood axed to kindling.

Then she paced at a distance while Angel crawled to her feet, good and mad. No one could tell what would happen next, and suddenly Angel launched herself like a rocket and flung her whole weight against Rowena with a mean doubled fist landing into her powerful jaw.

Which didn't faze Rowena too much. She pinned Angel's body to hers and commenced to squeeze.

'I never danced with dogshit before,' she grated out and tossed the winded fury away from her.

Angel hit the dust again, breathless and wild. Seemed she'd learned nothing when she went into the same bobcat spring, this time harder, this time thwacking into Rowena's neck with arm and elbow so Rowena choked and lost her balance and wound up sitting on the ground with Angel on her chest. She shook her off like so much road dirt and stood up again. This was business.

They recommenced weaving around until two things happened.

One was Assassina's arm flying to her thick hair and up into the air with a dangerous gleam; the other was a shot ringing out and Assassina's screamed curse as her hand dropped the deadly stiletto.

'Never expected dogshit and anythin' it was ridin' with

to fight anything but dirty,' said Rowena with distaste. 'You had enough, dogshit?'

Angel flung her hair back and snarled, '*No!*'

'Waaall, I have!' roared Rowena and in a lightning series of fist chops she appeared to tie Angel in knots so she wound up with both arms high behind her back, one leg pinned around the other and eating dirt.

'Dogshit,' said Rowena, holding her still. 'You're where you belong now. Don't you ever forget it. And don't you ever git none of your shithead buddies to draw a blade on the side of a fist fight. It ain't right.'

She stood up and walked back to her horse.

'Hey, dogshit's buddy – is your hand OK?'

She wasn't used to fighting outside a ring.

'The hand is fine,' said Mira. 'I shot the stiletto.'

'So – where are you heading?' said Grievous.

'Go fuck yourself, you goddam ass-licker,' said Mercedes, sucking the bullet burn. 'Come on, Angel, we got things to do.'

'What did she mean about a blade in the neck?' said Angel, glaring at me.

'Let's go!' screamed Assassina, and the pair pounded down the trail.

I told them about the stiletto I'd found in Suzanna's pillow.

'I should have gone for the heart,' said Mira, 'or the head – be on the safe side. We haven't seen the last of that pair.'

THIRTY-FOUR

Our spirits lit up and lifted the minute we cleared the western pass. Kimama lay ahead of us with those loose lazy-muscled flanks of hers like a beautiful woman who's just woken up and is real glad to see you. Seemed like nothing could change her, for all the ant-frantic scurryings and cesspit flurryings of Darknell von Doon and his cohorts.

Hell, we were on the way home!

Which meant seeing Roo again, for Mira.

For Grievous it was a chance to show off her big buddies to everyone and show off everyone to her big buddies.

It was a whole new adventure for Terry and Rowena, and the chance of a real major, crucial fight they could stage manage to their great big hearts' desire.

For me, back to Kimama was a lot of itchy waiting to see what would come our way in the mail. And, of course, it meant back to Suzanna. I smiled with a whole tantalizing body memory of when she'd hugged me goodbye and then stood, with those incredible blue eyes searching mine. We were both wary of words.

The horses were eager for home, too, and all at once a feeling of *yeeeeeee-ha!* shot through us all, and women and horses flew over the ground like birds off a lake at the sound of a gun.

And so to the house.

Suzanna was sitting dishevelled on the doorstep, and she and Fingerbone were matching each other from twin bottles of rotgut. They were deep in a philosophical analysis of the meaning of life.

'Motherfuckin' sons a bitches!' slurred Suzanna.

'Ain't I alwiz said the same?' growled Fingerbone. 'Hey – the girls are back!'

Suzanna turned her head a little unsteadily.

'Sent out three and come back with, lemme see – one . . . two, three – fucked if I don' see *ten* a you standin' there! Pished. Hi, Typewriter.' Her face broke into an extravagant grin. 'I'm drunk. As a skunk. Gonna shtay 'at way. Have a drink!'

I sat down and put my arm around her.

'Thass nice,' she said and leaned against me, a dead weight.

'We bin drinkin' since midday,' said Fingerbone, chuckling. 'We seen them crazy bitches offa the property, and hit it!'

'My liddle girl,' said Suzanna, a whisky tear splashing down her cheek. "S'all right. Be all right in the morning.'

She pillowed her head on my lap and snuggled in.

'Asleep?' said Mira.

I looked down at her dear, flushed face, her parted lips, the way her eyelashes were draped on her cheek.

'Yeah,' I said softly, and stroked her hair.

'She ain't been drunk in a age!' said Grievous. 'Hell, Fingerbone, whuchuh ben pourin' down her throat?'

'What's *she* ben pourin' down her own throat, yuh overmuscled sanctimone!' cackled Fingerbone. 'She needed tuh get good and drunk. She'll be brighter en a squerril in springtime come mornin'. Less git her to bed.'

'She's OK a while,' I said, real happy to have her lie across me the way she was.

Mira laughed.

'My God!' she said. 'It must be a good *friendship*. Typewriter, you know a sleeping drunk gets three pounds heavier every minute?' She ruffled my hair and started to hum a tune that sounded familiar. That German woman had been crooning it in Helga Klapperz bar the night before, and gotten encores by the dozen. Mira went into the house, and came out with a cushion she wiggled under me. Then she hauled a chair out against my back and the house wall.

'Waaall, Grievous, interdooss me tuh yuh frenz,' demanded Fingerbone with a leer.

'Goddam, where's mah manners! Terry, Rowena – the meanest gals you're ever like to see wrasslin' – this here is Mary Maloof Fingerbone. Gals, you know what the pair of you do in the ring by way of messin' each other up? Mary Maloof does the same thing inside only it's a fight between her guts and potato gin. So far, the guts is winnin'!'

'How do, ma'am,' said Terry and Rowena, who'd clearly been brought up to respect old age no matter what.

'Gonna call yuh Left and Right. I heard Grievous braggin' about the pair of yuh, and bein' identical, a'most. It's the gold teeth, ain't it?' said Fingerbone. The twins grinned.

Well, shortly, Grievous and her friends high-tailed off to do some regular exploring. Me and Mira and Fingerbone sat swilling a little hooch while Suzanna dozed on my knee and I let myself dream all those rose-pink candlelit thoughts I've taught myself never to admit to. Suddenly, she sat bolt upright.

'Jeeze Louise!' she exploded, coughing violently. 'Gimme a cigarette! What happened?'

'You just been washing away yuh blues, sugar,' said Fingerbone. 'Time yuh took yuh sweet self a nap.'

'Uh-huh,' said Suzanna, drawing on the smoke I'd built for her, then wincing upright. 'I'll see yuh later.'

I stood up too.

'I don' need no help,' she grumbled, stumbling to sprawl face down on the porch. I hoisted her up and listened to the litany of *she-din-need-no-assistance*, god*dam* it, all the way upstairs. She fell on her bed. Well, I pulled off her boots and commenced undressing her, first in the interests of a comfortable sleep, but I swear, when she was down to her lovely nakedness, I had a bad case of tingling skin and hot flushes. Ah, well! I rolled her into bed, and her eyelids fluttered. She reached up to me and held me close.

''S good to see you, honey,' she slurred. 'I'll let you know how good . . . mm, later.'

I like to see people drunk. You always know the shit from the honey then. When you're drunk it's like peeling the layers off, and God, do you ever find what folk would rather hide! But with a real person, you just get an exaggerated view of how they are anyway. I kissed my saint on her sleeping brow and stole away.

'That was quick,' said Mira with a wicked grin, and set to whistling that tune again.

'Whutchuh whistling there, Europe?' said Fingerbone to Mira, like sometimes she called me East Coast, and Suzanna Miz Lofty Britches outta Nowhere.

'"Falling In Love Again",' said Mira. 'Seems to be on my mind right now.'

Fingerbone kicked me. From her, that was approval. 'Orright, ain't she, this overeddicated eastern bitch?'

'Seems OK with Suzanna. OK with me. OK with all of us,' said Mira, with a throaty laugh.

I let myself bask a little. Falling in love again? I allowed the phrase to stroll around my mind. Falling in *love* again? Maybe. What else have I ever done in this mess called life that's brought me real joy?

THIRTY-FIVE

We allowed that it was night when Fingerbone's snores shattered the blissful dark. Mira squeezed my shoulder, Grievous wished me sweet dreams, and I was left alone to the house. I pulled a rug over Fingerbone, and eased her empty flask to the boards by her feet.

Alone.

In the dark.

The sky above was littered with rhinestone constellations, the air was busy with heady scents and the heavy insistent whirring of moon-rainbowed insects. I sipped at the last sweet half-inch of bourbon: not drunk, but not so sober that life felt anything other than delicious, promising scents, tantalizing me the way the five-and-dime candy counter had me wide-eyed and tongue-tied on tiptoe every Saturday when I was a kid.

I shoved my hands in my pockets and slouched upstairs like I was simply going to bed. It was the landing had me dithering and foolish. *To bed, to bed, sleepy-head!* But my shadow stretched out along the floor to where Suzanna's half-closed, half-open door drew me. Sure, she was asleep. Passed out. Hadn't I put her to bed hours before? But the memory of the sheer warmth of her sleeping skin tugged at me. My whole body ached with desire for sleep-heat, the half-awake turning of my body next to hers, the casual dream-depths of an arm – hers! – flung around me; the waking moments when I saw for sure the moonlit curves of her cheeks and brow, the splash of a stray moonbeam carving her unique lips to a thing of eternal beauty . . .

How could I do anything but peel off my boots and tiptoe along the silvered beams of the floor that led to her? My feet padded to the knowing creak of old boards and swept me into the womb-darkness and warmth where she was deep asleep.

There she lay. Suzanna. Goddess of my wildest dreams. I shed my clothes the way a tree shakes off its leaves, anticipating the sure and glorious blanket of winter, the sparkle of frost. I slid in beside her: the edge of the bed was chill, but her body had kissed the sheets with a glow of human warmth. I waited for my heart to beat slow as natural, tensed against the moment I would stop shivering, cold and longing forcing a whiplash brake of numbness on me.

Finally I was relaxed. As relaxed as I could be when Suzanna was only a heartbeat away. I inched myself towards her sleeping body, and glided my arm around her. She moved and clasped my hand to her breast. I melted into her heat and we slept, my mouth wide in wonder at the nape of her neck.

Came morning.

We were still in the intense embrace of sleeping. Was she awake?

'Hey,' she murmured, 'was I awful?'

'You were fine,' I said to her neck. 'Drunk, but very fine.'

She sighed a little.

'Is it real early?' she said. 'I mean, as early as I feel?' Then she threw her head back on my arm and laughed. 'Stupid question!' she said. 'This lazy old bitch can't even get up to see the daylight!' But then she swung out of bed and parted the curtains. 'Damn!' she said breathlessly. 'The frost's setting like a crown on the grass, and there's mist all over. You want to ride?'

Anything to share the thrill in her voice. We dressed hastily, like we were running away, and by the door I held her close.

'Go-od!' she said. 'You are one warm woman, Helena. I'd almost forgotten that bit. Later. OK?'

Everything was OK as she kissed me. And she'd used my real name for the first time. I died and went to join the angels. Came the resurrection as she fixed strong coffee that scalded my lips. Me and my halo and wings crunched through the grass beside her and we saddled up Snow and Dawn, my mare.

'I'm going to take you somewhere you've never been before. Only me and Rainbow-Wings know about it. Let's go!'

It was like flying, the way the horses breasted the early mist clear across the valley. My cheeks stung with cold, then heat leaped in, and the sun capped the peaks of Kimama with light, the rocks above us stood out above the grey foothills. As we rode, the cape of light rippled downwards the way the folds of a balldress fall to the floor, and the mist was tugged from the grass in swift gusts. The edge of the shadow of the valley rushed to meet us and we reined in the horses in the full crisp chill of autumn sunshine.

'Are you OK?' said Suzanna.

My grin said more than any words could.

'Go Snow!' she whooped, and our hooves spun catherine wheels of bright dew through the turf.

As the land sloped upwards, she slowed, and we picked our way more carefully towards the line of spruce and cottonwoods.

'Better walk from here,' she said. 'We'll leave Snow and Dawn free to graze. She knows my whistle.'

We knotted the reins over the horses' necks and plunged into the tawny bracken, a maze of frost-blue lichened twigs snapping under our feet. In the undergrowth, scarlet berries shone like forbidden jewels; fantastic twists and whorls of fungi burst from fallen logs. Suzanna ducked branches and sprung up half-mossed rocky scars, grabbing at lithe twigs that switched right back to my hand for me to follow.

The ground rose so steeply, thick with fallen leaves, there was nothing to hold on to in the autumn-soaked softness of earth. The only way up was to fling ourselves full length and dig toes and fingers deep, sliding backwards near as much as we went forwards, caterpillaring along the slippery leaves. We were all over mud and broken leaves when the land condescended a dip wide enough to sprawl on. But not for long – the edge threatened to crumble and we scrambled up again, where rocks gave handholds, and places to kick off with our feet.

Then we reached an illusory peak; foothills have a way of lifting, then falling, in massive sculpted ripples. We were on a grassy saddle of land that rolled away to another deep mesa and the next ridge was higher, the next valley would be steeper. Above us, the mountain swept up to the sky.

'Are we going right up there?' I asked Suzanna.

She stood gazing high, eyes narrowed against the brilliant sky.

'No one's ever been up there, sweetheart,' she said. 'It's the kind of place you could lose yourself in – for years, even. Rainbow-Wings told me there was a legend among her people about a wise woman who went all the way up there. When she came back, everyone she'd known was dead, and her own great-granddaughter, who hadn't even been born when she went up the mountain – she was a hundred and seven years old. Rainbow-Wings reckons time gets spirited away high in the mountains.'

THIRTY-SIX

'So where are we going?' I asked. Suzanna's grin burst into a laugh.

'I ain't about to tell you,' she teased. 'It's a secret.'

'Aw, come on!' I said, and she shook her head, her eyes dancing. God, she was lovely! What to do with this good feeling? I lunged towards her and knocked her flying, sat on her stomach and pinned her arms to the ground.

'You don't get let up till you tell,' I said.

'The hell I don't!' she gasped, laughing and struggling till I lost balance and we rolled over and over like kids in the snow. We fetched up against a rock, breathlessly face to face.

'You want a kiss or you want to know where we're going?'

'Yeah,' I said looking up at her.

'Well, you're certainly getting kissed, woman, and you'll just have to trust me for the rest.'

No question that I did, as our lips met softly, nuzzled so gently then with wildfire longing like we were starving.

'Later!' she said with a fierce moan. 'Christ Jesus! It's been a long time for me, Helena. Just give me some time. Let's take it slow.'

And who was I to bitch about giving her time, when my heart and soul and the rest of my life were already gift-wrapped and tagged with her name?

'Come on then,' she said, tugging me upright and

133

striding across the grass, still holding my hand. 'Look. See the stones?'

She pointed ahead to where the grassy swathe of land was studded with rocks and stones thick as a daisy meadow.

'The Indians put them here – before time began, says Rainbow-Wings. Each one means something: there's stars and maps and animals here, and each pattern points you along a path. The animals show the way to good hunting; the stars point you all over: the way of meditation, the way of mourning a loss, the way to all kind of spirits, the way of change. See?'

I could pick out a horse's head, the head of a buffalo, a spiral –

'What's the spiral?'

'That's the forbidden way – the way up the mountain. It closes back into itself endlessly, leading nowhere, leading everywhere. Jeeze! you shoulda heard Rainbow-Wings tell it.'

'Which way are we taking?'

'My, my, don't she ask a lot of questions?' said Suzanna, shaking her head. 'The way we're taking is called wait-and-see. Come on!'

We walked slowly through the patterns until we came to a curve of grass double-bordered by white stones gleaming with quartz. Suzanna walked ahead on the narrow strip and I followed. There was a sudden burst of birdsong nearby, and a streak of kingfisher-blue feathers in the trees.

'Jay,' said Suzanna. 'That's good.'

Our path wound in intricate curves, looping back on itself, white stones sweeping across other patterns, leading away towards the woods, then back to the studded turf of the hilltop. Gradually the stones spread wider so we could walk side by side, and further apart until there were five, six, then ten paces between each one and we were led to the edge of the trees. I stopped still and touched Suzanna's arm, pointing to where a fine-antlered deer was poised motionless not ten yards from us.

She smiled and nodded.

'That's a tree,' she said softly. 'Nothing here is what it seems.'

Yes, it was a tree, and the deer's dark eye was a deep-cored bole in the wood, the antlers were bare mossed branches.

'And you ain't seen nothing yet!' said Suzanna, her voice proud with promise. The trees gave way to a forest of upright stones, their cracks strung with spider webs; slow fingers of ivy tipped with tender green leaves crept upwards in zigzags. We came to the tallest stone.

'Close your eyes,' said Suzanna, and took my hand, guiding me a few steps on. 'Now – open!'

The earth dropped away at my feet and I was gazing at the strangest sight I have ever seen.

It was as if someone the size of a mountain had scooped up a handful of earth and left a raw red dip, where the sides were gouged by giant fingers, and the floor was smooth as rock. Upright red and orange and umber and tan rocks stood there like pieces of an interrupted chess game. But though they were stone, there was a roseate softness in them that made me want to be close enough to touch. Without a word, Suzanna slid over the edge and me after her. One dizzy look was enough, as we spread-eagled our way along narrow ledges even as steps. My back felt naked and prickled with a feeling of being watched, but I wanted to look behind me and meet this look, for it felt like a welcome.

It was so far to the ground that I slipped into a floating dream of moving, until Suzanna nudged me.

'We're here,' she said, and we turned and slid into sitting, the strange rocks towering above us, tall as trees.

Without a word we rose and wandered apart, lost sight of each other in the forest colonnade: each rock blocked out another, and the sky above was bitten into by the tips of the columns like shifting jigsaw pieces. My feet were soundless on the ground, shifting only a little dust that rose and settled into grooves raked neat as gravel. I leaned against one pillar and drank in the whorls and fine cracks delicate as an ancient hand-drawn map. There was a hush all around, so much was there no sound I could feel it on my face like the dream of a cobweb in the dark.

And so I wandered through this maze, stopping to stare at this rock or that, sitting back against rocks curved to fit my back, and at these my eyes would be drawn to a particular point where I could see a bird, a tree, a cloud, a horse, seemingly carved, but close to, nothing more or less than a fabulous accident of colouring or shadow or contour.

'He-ey!'

Came Suzanna's voice, ricocheting around the place, sliding and changing note so I was chorused by echoes in this petrified wood. The sound stirred me, led me dipping and weaving wherever it went until I fetched up against Suzanna standing with her back to me on the other side of the rocks.

'My voice will still be here when we go back through,' she said. 'The stones never let go of a sound. You try.'

I threw my head back and let out a whoop. Suddenly wondered if that was like dancing in church but the stones seized it and flung it around like a ball.

And then we were off again, through a deep mossed gully out of sight of the rocks, a frantic scramble up stream-splashed rocks, and all the time Suzanna glancing back at me with a sense of urgency that had me forcing myself to the limit. She paused for a moment at a pool caught in the rocks where a cascade of water drummed endlessly on the dark surface. But then she hurtled up the side of the fall like a cat and finally turned to catch my hand and haul me onto a high ledge where we lay gasping.

'Now,' she said. 'Look!'

She was pointing at the water where a jagged rock stuck

through the silver sheet. There burned a rainbow of pure light that shifted unwaveringly wherever I moved my head.

'Rainbow-Wings was born here,' said Suzanna.

'She said she was born the other side of the valley,' I said.

'That's because she didn't know you. That's the place she's chosen to live – a sort of second birthplace. I feel like I was born in Kimama some days. I can almost see myself in a cradle in the corner of the kitchen sometimes,' said Suzanna, then laughed at herself. 'Hell, there are times I think Rainbow-Wings is nuts, but times like here it all makes sense to me.'

We ate bread and cheese as the sun reached its zenith, then Suzanna sighed and smiled, putting her hand on my arm.

'Maybe I'm nuts too,' she said. 'The Lord knows I ought to be back at the house, figuring out this god-almighty mess we got. But it seemed the right thing coming here with you today.'

Mention of van Doon sobered the day and we went back more quickly than either of us wanted: me, I'd have stayed days and nights there, and I think Suzanna would have too.

All too soon we were back at the house, and Suzanna went off to find Grievous and Lucille.

I went and sat in the study, staring at a piece of paper, closing my eyes to see the rich whirl of images she and the day had brought me. Slowly, the sun set and I lit the lamp.

Then in the peach glow of light, I found myself writing a poem for Suzanna. I am not the poem type, and even if I still had it, I wouldn't put it in here. Not now. I have this thing about love letters, and my poem was a love letter. For her eyes only. I seem to remember parts of it, no doubt the sun had risen by the second line, there was probably autumn gold and a harvest moon besides, certainly there were eyes of ocean blue, kisses too, and probably breakers on a sea shore. And trees, spring trees, waterfalls and magic.

All of which was me trying to say to her in words what my body expressed with her in every touch; it was setting the feeling of now in the eternal amber of love. Amber, ambrosia, the minutes were liquid gold. So I gave her the poem by firelight late that night, staying the delicious moment when our flesh would touch and say it all surely and so much better.

She read to my heartbeat and the crackling logs, violet bark flakes curling to neon, whispering down to ash.

'I don't know what to say,' she said, rubbing her jaw hard as if she could find and force out the words that way. 'No one's ever written me poems before.'

And why not? raged my proud heart, then, to clear her embarrassment, I said something about what do you expect from a writer.

She looked into my eyes, her whole life playing across the stormy grey-blue. God, how I loved her.

'Let's go to bed,' she said, pulling me to my feet. We took the stairway to heaven.

And though I didn't know it at the time – and who the hell ever does? – that was the best day I would ever spend with Suzanna of Kimama.

THIRTY-SEVEN

Rainbow-Wings by the Rushing Waters sat huddled by the falls waiting for a rush of rainbow wings, the coming of the butterflies. They breathed life to her home, Kimama, and this year they were late.

Lariat Lucille sat by her, the pair of them mother-naked as so many times before. Rainbow-Wings, had she used the word, *loved* Lariat Lucille, had *loved* her from the minute Lucille's lips had parted on a wry gold-toothed grin some 169 moons before. Lariat Lucille had *loved* Rainbow-Wings the minute she saw her move like a wild chestnut grulla through the silver-birch grove above the falls.

It had nothing to do with words.

I love you.

Ah *lerve* yew!

Yew air th' only one for me!

All of this was fool's gold compared with the twenty-carat vein running between Lucille and Rainbow-Wings by the Rushing Waters.

Lariat Lucille picked up a worry as her lover's body shivered. Was it the butterflies? No. That would be a joyous thrill. Two days they had sat and slept and fasted by the tumbling waters. And no shimmering myriad cloud on any horizon. Instead, as she looked up, a cloud full of rain bit cold chunks of sky from the path of the sun, turning it into the rolling glare of a chill white eye through miasmic grey.

But in the sudden cold, a distant hum thrilled them to the core.

Rainbow-Wings leaped up and scried the skies.

'A bird!' she breathed.

But what a bird!

Even so high and far away, it was the size of a bird you might see perched on a mess of twigs in the cliffs a spit ahead of you. And with it came an insistent hum growling louder to a roar. The bird grew bigger and hurtled over them, its wings stiff, its body rigid.

Their eyes met, they shucked on clothes and scrambled downstream, tore past the house and down to the plain, with a gut-throbbing, ear-splitting metallic noise overhead.

A shot rang out. The bull roar of Mary Maloof's twelve-bore.

'Fingerbone!' burst out Lariat Lucille, diving back to the

house where, sure enough, the old lady was tottered upright and aiming her ancient barrels at the heavens.

'Don't shoot!' gasped Lucille. 'Me Old China knows what's going on!'

'Air yew sure?' rasped Fingerbone, lowering her sights. 'I hear a thing sounds like a plague of locusts, looks like a goddam eagle and bigger en a damn house – *Me Old China knows* about it?'

'Sure,' said Lucille, scarlet from running. 'It's something to do with the butterflies.'

'Ha!' said the old woman warily. 'Waaall, okee! On'y I got mah trigger cocked here in case yew pair need a little lead to help the magic along.'

Lucille went pelting down to the plain with me and Grievous and Roo close behind her. The danged bird, or whatever it might be, was getting lower now, flying in great smooth sweeps. Then it landed on the grass, ran ahead a little and stopped. The noise stopped too, and my ears rang with the silence.

What in the hell was it? You could go a long way round and never get to describing it. It was all white and shiny like paint on the outside. The wings stayed stiff, like a great bird been pinned still. There was a round nose nothing like a beak. The head was kind of squashed-looking with two huge flat glassy eyes. All at once these eye-panels flung outwards, causing us all to draw. What the hell was going on? But a human figure jumped out of each eye and both walked round to the squashed beak, grinning like angels or happy fools come straight from lulu land.

THIRTY-EIGHT

'Good thing we found this strip to land on,' said one of them, peeling a leather helmet off short dark hair. 'Damned if I know how the fuel's gotten us this far anyhow.'

'Amelia, you know that fuel gauge has been on zero from the minute we took off. I figure the needle's broken. Either that or this is a stunt for a new wonder fuel. Hi there, folks!'

The last was a cheery wide smile as they got to where we were, all busy shoving our rods away with some embarrassment. These were women after all, if we knew nothing else about the two people who'd dropped down here out of a clear sky.

Grievous stepped forward.

'What in the hail is that thing?' she said, pointing to the big bird behind them.

'Neat, isn't she? *Vega*. Nothing flies better, never has,' said one of the women.

'Vega, huh?' said Grievous, with the same deep suspicion she'd shown towards my typewriter.

'Is it a bird, or what?' said Rainbow-Wings by the Rushing Waters.

'Helluva big bird,' said the other, older woman, with an easy laugh.

'Well, *what is it*?' said Rainbow-Wings with a firebrand intensity that made the older woman step back two paces.

'Hey, ease up, honey,' she said. 'It's an aeroplane. You never seen one before?'

'No,' said Rainbow-Wings.

'I'll be hanged and my horse too!' said the older woman. 'Where have you been?'

'Here,' said Rainbow-Wings. 'Kimama.'

'That's the name kept coming to us,' said the younger woman excitedly. 'You remember, Neta? Tried to work out where it had come from – you thought it was some Mexican card game? This place is called Kimama?'

'Yeah,' said Grievous. 'Tho' we appear to be set to play more en a game of poker here. Whut is it, this airy-plane? Whassit do?'

'Well, honey, it flies like a bird,' said the younger woman. 'You just get in and switch on and wh-oooooooom! you're in the air.'

'Aw, bullshit!' protested Grievous.

'No bullshit!' she said. 'You want a ride?'

'Yurrr!' said Grievous, the way she was squaring up to a regular brawl.

'Well, come on in then,' said the younger woman, and they strode to this aeroplane, big bird, humming monster.

'Sorry, folks,' said the older woman, running a tanned hand through her salt-and-pepper hair, 'Amelia always takes a challenge.'

'So does Grievous,' said Roo pleasantly.

'We'd better get out of the way,' said the older woman, as the hanging feathers on the big bird's wings started to whirr around.

The bird roared past us, and lifted off the ground.

'Grievous is *inside* that thing?' said Lucille, grabbing her hat against the sudden wind.

Only the stranger and Rainbow-Wings stayed upright as the aeroplane passed overhead. She stood proud and tall as a tree, one muscled hand shading her brow against the blazing sun.

'Wings of metal,' she breathed, her whole body thrilling as the 'bird' shot towards the western pass.

'Is that a good thing, honey?' said Lariat Lucille.

'It's what we need,' said Rainbow-Wings.

The plane landed again and rolled to a halt. Grievous swung out to the ground and every eye was on her as she walked towards us. She stopped, looked at us the way you do when you've had a vision, tore her hat off and stamped on it, grinning like a sanctified fool.

'Damn!' she exploded. 'Why wasn't I told before? I just ben up with the birdies and the angels, hell, we even ben thru' a *cloud*! Ben so all-fired close tuh the treetops I coulda reached down and broke off the topmost twig to prove it! Yuh know how it is when you're in the hills and can see everywhere? It's better en that! We ben tuh the top of the sky! Hell, it's *flyin'*!'

Amelia caught up with her, smiling real proud and delighted, but trying not to show it too much.

'Anyone else?' she said.

There was no question but Rainbow-Wings must be next. Her whole body thrilled as she strode to the machine with Amelia.

We sat watching them go, then turned to Grievous for more.

'I jest cain't explain!' she kept saying, shaking her head. Neta Snook put an arm around her shoulders.

'That's always the way the first time you go up,' she said. 'You've never seen a plane before either – God knows how! I been hoboing round in the air ever since I can remember. First plane I saw I knew I had to fly. Spent more time in the air than on the ground ever since.'

'What's going on?' The voice carved its way between us.

THIRTY-NINE

It was Suzanna. I looked up at her with that fond and foolish smile I couldn't seem to avoid around her, but her eyes were on Neta Snook.

'Aw, Suzanna, you shoulda been here!' said Grievous. 'I ben flying. In th' air. Like a damn bird.'

Suzanna had that imperious reserve she'd shown to me when I first arrived.

'I'm Neta Snook' said the new woman, rising and extending a gauntleted hand.

'Suzanna LaReine,' said she, with a brisk handshake. 'What brings you here?'

'Damned if I know!' said Neta with an infectious grin. 'This is where the wind blew us, and there wasn't a thing we could do to alter the course. Kimama, huh?'

'Yes,' said Suzanna carefully, 'Kimama. What – brings you here? How did you get here?'

'They come in an airy-plane, Suzanna,' said Grievous. 'Aw, yuh'll have tuh wait till Rainbow-Wings and Amelia come down again. Blamed if I kin explain!'

'Come *down*?' said Suzanna, looking at all of us. 'They've gone *up* some place?'

'Up in the air!' said Grievous.

Suzanna looked pained. 'You're talking crazy,' she said.

'Rainbow-Wings knows all about it, Suzanna,' said Lucille. 'It's a flying bird made out of metal. I'd have said it was crazy talk, if I hadn't seen it with my own eyes.'

'Hmm,' said Suzanna, folding her arms, more than a little put out, then alarmed as the roar of the plane came hammering out of the distance. She flattened her hat to her head as the wings swept low over us and the machine bumped down onto the grass, then majestically wheeled our way. Rainbow-Wings leaped to the ground and pelted towards us.

'This is it, Suzanna!' she cried. 'Strike me pink! We went up over the pass like a bleedin' eagle! Floated over Swallerin' Gulch like a buzzard! And back again! This is *it*!'

'You went to Swallering Gulch and back?' said Suzanna, lifting one eyebrow. 'Come *on*, Me Old China, pull the other one.'

'Straight up, Suzanna, you try and see for yourself.'

'Hi!' said Amelia to Suzanna. 'Are you next?'

Suzanna was less than pleased at this familiarity.

'This is Suzanna LaReine,' said Neta Snook, 'Amelia Earhardt. I figure this is your outfit, Suzanna? Amelia, she'd like to know how we got here. What we're doing here.'

'Blessed if I know!' said Amelia, chuckling. 'This has been the strangest flight ever. I hardly needed to look at the instruments – the plane flew herself here.'

'Hmm,' said Suzanna, weighing up the strangers, then, 'What are we waiting for? Let's go *up*!'

'Ef she ain't one uppity bitch!' hissed Fingerbone as Suzanna led the way to the plane.

'You see, mate,' said Rainbow-Wings to Neta Snook, 'we've got a spot of bother. More like a ruddy carbuncle. This is Suzanna's gaff, this valley.'

'It's a beautiful place,' said Neta, gazing around as the plane hurtled past us and into the air.

Rainbow-Wings gave her a brief run-down on Darknell van Doon and his cattle syndicate, then launched into a lyrical description of her vision of metal wings by way of the butterflies that were late this year, from whom the valley got its name. It was Neta's turn to look puzzled.

'Is that strictly legal? You can't just have a shoot-out! Not these days!'

'Eynd whah *not*?' said Grievous. 'Yuh tell me a better way to protect your home!'

'Well, what do your menfolk think?' said Neta. 'Most places I've been, men run the show; hell, I had to fight 'em even to get in the seat of a plane. Fight my father, my brothers, lose my fiancé . . .'

'We seem to get by without men in Kimama,' drawled Mira.

'No men at all?'

'Nope,' said Grievous. 'We ain't never missed 'em, side from thangs being a heap more sane and happy en when they're struttin' around givin' orders.'

'Well, that makes life a deal simpler,' said Neta. 'But I don't see where we – me and Amelia and *Vega* – where do we come in?'

Rainbow-Wings smiled serenely. 'With your skills, with

your metal bird, we can see for miles. It's a way of seeing the future. By the time van Doon and his men set out on the road from Swallering Gulch to here, we've seen them and got back. We can't be surprised.'

'Sides to that,' said Grievous, 'they's a hatchway in yuh airy-plane. Wouldn't hurt us none to drop a few thangs outta it onto they cussed pizen heads!'

'You're talking war!' said Neta, alarmed.

'It's us or them,' said Lucille, 'ain't it, Typewriter? Tell her!'

'Darknell van Doon,' I said, 'is a murdering, lying, cheating, fire-raising, wheeling-dealing, sewer-bred bastard, gives bastards a bad name and sewers too. He's set on bankrupting a bunch of innocent investors and wiping us out to line his jackal-hide wallet. He's got to be stopped.'

'You don't like him a whole heap, do you?' said Neta.

'I wouldn't piss on his face in the desert,' I said.

'Waall? Air yuh with us?' said Grievous.

'I'll have to talk to Amelia,' said Neta.

'You'll both have to talk to Suzanna,' I said.

We all scanned the empty blue sky.

FORTY

There was something Suzanna wasn't happy about, though Rainbow-Wings's face shone with inspiration. On the way back to the house, Mary Maloof puffed along beside me, well behind the rest, and put me wise.

'Yuh know what's botherin' Miz Proud-As-Satan, Typewriter?' she wheezed. 'Course yuh don't! Right now the sun's shinin' outta her asshole as far as yew kin see, which ain't the distance a two-leg mule kin hobble! Nah! Sweet Sue's got that purdy nose booted outta joint cuz she ain't the *first* tuh see thet blamed airy-plane! Lahks tuh imagine she gotta put the seal of approval on ever' dam thang comes this way! Hah! Got to be the first, and the best in everythang she does! Yuh never see that side a' her yit, do yuh, Typewriter? Aw, she'll let 'em stay, seein' as how y'all are so set on it, and she trusts Grievous so whut Grievous says goes. Heh! Ah'd lahk tuh be in thet theer airy-plane and drop a mess a' stuff on thet stuffed-britches onterprenoor mahself! Yuh keep a eye out fuh Sweet Sue, Typewriter. I ain't long fuh this world, mahself. Nuthin' I kin do to help matters, so I wind up prayin' – me, Typewriter, I pray and don't nuthin' happen! Goddam Rainbow-Wings has herself a dream and it comes true! They ain't no justice!'

Well, dinner that night found Sweet Sue, Suzanna LaReine, the love of my life, showing a steel core I knew was there but had never witnessed. She made it sound like she didn't give too much of a damn if Neta and Amelia and their bird-machine stayed or not. When they said they'd like to, she smiled and said only:

'I leave all that to Rainbow-Wings and Lucille. The next coupla weeks gonna be work from dawn to midnight. What I've seen in Swallering Gulch today is bad. They've set up a practice range and got a hunnerd or so firin' at it. I seen that cutesy little surrey settin' in Main Street besides. Van Doon's getting ready to strike.'

'You must have eagle eyes!' said Amelia admiringly. 'We were flying high enough! All I could see was streets!'

Suzanna shrugged. She had seen more. But what?

'I know what I'm looking for,' she said, smiling grimly. 'And I saw it. Trouble. Tomorrow we start and we'll make trouble like van Doon's having nightmares about, if dirt can dream.'

Amelia and Neta went down to the bunkhouse with the crew, and Suzanna ground her cheroot out, half smoked. She lashed bourbon into a couple of glasses and slouched into the biggest chair by the fire. I took the one opposite.

'What do *you* think, Typewriter?' she said, moodily.

'I want to know what else you saw from that plane.'

'I wish you'd been there,' she said. 'I used a pair of eye-glasses Amelia had in the plane. Horseshit do I have eagle eyes! I seen Miz van Doon having herself a parasol promenade.'

'And?'

'Two guesses who she's using for company?'

'Give up.'

'Mercedes Assassina, that's goddam who! And Angel Star, my flesh and blood, all arm in arm like a nest of tarantulas! You know what that means? Means all our secrets are out. This old bitch is fool enough to let Angel in on the secret ways to Kimama, blood being thicker than water! One *stupid* old bitch I am! Setting alongside one young woman done more in her life than I've dreamed of or dared, and looking down on my own whelp doing stuff I'd never be so low as to consider! You know what I felt in that machine? I felt *old*!'

Suzanna smashed her fist into the chair, and flung a furious flame at her cheroot. I wished there was something I could say.

'And Grievous's got herself two young women with more muscle in one arm than I have in my body!'

'But we're all working together, Suzanna,' I said.

'Yeah,' she said. 'I just recall the days when it was me holed up and shooting my own way outta anything they could throw at me! Damn! Those were the days! I feel useless. Old and useless.'

'And these are the days,' I said. 'You think anyone would be bothering to defend this place if you hadn't made it what we all want? Wise up, Suzanna. Any one of us would just grab herself a decent horse and light out of here. Put us all together and you've got a different story. Everyone's got different reasons for wanting to be here, but all those reasons are tied up with you like the breath in our bodies. You've made it all possible.'

'Huh!' said Suzanna, gulping bourbon.

I wondered if it would make a difference, saying what was on my mind. I could hardly bear to see her so grim.

'Why do you think I'm here, Suzanna? What the hell can I do against van Doon?'

'You wrote them letters. That's what you do best,' she said morosely. 'Who knows, that might have some effect.'

I cursed my tied tongue.

'Anyhow, Typewriter, you didn't come here to fight a frontier war. I thought you'd be up and off – what did you say? – ahead of what they like to call civilization? I like that idea.'

'You think I could leave *now*?' I said, willing her to look at me. She slumped lower in the chair. There was nothing else for it.

'Suzanna, I love you,' I said, suddenly finding myself fascinated by the way the logs were blazing. A million-year silence sat between us.

'Love?' said Suzanna. 'Aw, Jesus. I wish you hadn't said that.'

I melted. Took her hand.

'But it's true,' I said. 'How could I not love you? Aren't you Suzanna LaReine?'

She squeezed my hand and put it back on my knee. 'Love,' she said, closing her eyes. 'That's one tiny word means things so huge it scares the shit outta me.'

But surely not now! Surely not with me!

'I've tripped over that word and fell flat on my face more times than the summer fool that's blindfolded to stumble through a fresh-ploughed field to give folk something to laugh at! Love!'

I was frozen.

'Oh, forget it,' I said, forcing my voice to normal. 'Forget I ever said it.'

'You have a perfect right to say it,' she said. 'Just wish you hadn't. That's all. Give me time, Typewriter. Let me get this mess sorted out. Give this old bitch time.'

The logs ashed in our silence.

'You think I can forget anything you say?' Suzanna said suddenly. 'When your words have saved my life? I never forget anything you say.'

I built a smoke, cursing my trembling hands. *Boy, did you ever fuck up!* I raged.

Suzanna reached over and stroked my hair.

'What was it Rainbow-Wings called you? Fools Rush In? Y'see, you can do that, Typewriter, God knows how, you can just up and do stuff and say stuff I'd never let pass my lips. I don't have the right way. You don't have the right way. But I know me, and love sure ain't highlighted on my path. I'm so sorry. I wish I was different. I wish everything in my life was different. But it ain't.'

'No,' I said, curling up inside like a butterfly that never managed to make it through the chrysalis stage.

'Oh, Jesus!' said Suzanna, killing her bourbon. 'Why the hell not? I just wish you'd hit me or something and make it easier. For me. I tried to kid myself we were just having a good time. I kinda knew it was different for you. Didn't want to think about it, tell the truth. Shit! Just give me time. OK?'

'Suzanna,' I said, holding her hand again, 'you want time, you've got it. What else was I doing when I met you? You think I was looking to be in love? What difference does time make to me when I'm near you? You want time – you've got it, darling. All the time you want.'

She smiled and we downed another inch or so of bourbon.

And so to bed.

We shared a bed that night. But love lay between us, warmth handcuffing me against holding her, where snowbound fear kept her apart. In the morning we held each other, the tasks of the day throwing their own chains around us both.

'It'll work out, Typewriter,' she said, kissing my brow. 'Can you stand it?'

I had no choice, but that was better than nothing.

'Sure,' I said. 'You'll know when I can't. I just won't be here.'

FORTY-ONE

By the mirror, I stopped and looked myself straight in the eye. I had a sick feeling of dread and cursed that I hadn't kept my mouth shut the night before. But there is no right time to say 'I love you' if it's the wrong thing to say. Like, if someone really doesn't want to hear it. Hell, I could always leave. Why break the habits of a lifetime? Congratulations, asshole, I told my grim reflection, and took extra care dressing, like I didn't give a damn. There is nothing less attractive than a lovesick fool with a hangdog expression. I pinned on a silver brooch of a gun intertwined with a whip: a present from Hal Mayflower-Ames for a story damn nearly got me killed. Some things I feel good remembering, some things I've done right. So – Suzanna wasn't in love with me. I told myself it was her loss, and hoped for the day when I'd either believe it or simply not care.

Downstairs she surprised me with a huge smile and a hug. 'You're OK, Typewriter,' she said.

Well, maybe it wasn't so bad, after all. Maybe she did just want time. I put all my thoughts on ice in the bustle of the day.

Breakfast was a reckless open-air picnic, while we organized who would do what. Suzanna strolled around looking preoccupied, listening to all the plans with a nod and a grim twist of the lips. We all knew firepower alone wouldn't take the dozen or so of us far against van Doon and his paid cohorts.

Grievous and the twins aimed on heading west to do a little damming to divert the foothill streams to where they would soak the ground and build a mud-wallow right across the plain by way of a welcome mat. Then they would commence to shovelling deep covered trenches and laying trip wires over the wooded paths Suzanna was cursing she'd let Angel know about. The twins were trying to figure out a way of causing an avalanche on the narrowest part of the pass besides.

'Jest a few real big rocks!' they pleaded when Grievous hummed and hawed about would there be time. 'We kin always clear it up afterwards!'

Suzanna laughed in spite of herself. 'Aw, come on, Momma Grievous, let the kiddies have some fun. Go for it, girls! You'd think this was a children's tea party hearing you two!'

'No point frettin' ourselves to miserable afore we have to,' said Terry.

The three of them whooped off in the bright sunshine.

Rainbow-Wings and Lucille were deep in conversation with Amelia and Neta, their idea being to fill the plane with as many things as it would take and drop them from a great height on the crawling column below. Suzanna sat on her heels beside them.

'What sort of *things*, Lucille?'

'Things,' said Lucille. 'Odd objects, Suzanna. Stuff like all the trash we been shoving outta sight in the cellar and the sheds.'

'Would be good to do some spring cleaning,' said Grits. 'We got no use fer them thangs – mah ole sewin' machine fer one. She's heavy as a cow. Don't nobody fixed her yit nor likely to. Thet'd surprise 'em. Might even knock 'em cold! And them rusty ole billycans! Fill 'em up with stones! Sides, I'm gonna bake me a batch of bread without no yeast, this very day as is. Bread like Fingerbone bakes. Tooth-breakin' bread! Haid-breakin' too if yuh wuz to aim right! Heh! I'll git to it!'

'What yuh say about mah bakin'?' threatened Fingerbone.

'I said yuh kin give me a hand today, old lady. Make

yuhself useful. No one bakes like you! Y' can tell me the secret.'

'Praise be!' crowed Fingerbone. 'See, Suzanna, someone round here do appreciate good home cookin'!'

'God almighty!' said Suzanna sarcastically. 'Anyone round here got time enough on their hands to clean a few guns? In the event we need to blow away the lucky few don't get swamped or tripped or knocked out by flying loaves and billycans? Jesus!'

'Yup,' said Roo, 'I'm with you.'

'Me too,' said Mira. 'Don't look so desperate, Suzanna. This thing is just about crazy enough to work.'

'I'll give you a hand,' I said. 'I have been known to handle a gun.'

'No,' said Rainbow-Wings suddenly. 'Someone has to go to the falls, and Fools Rush In knows the spot to watch from.'

'Yeah,' said Suzanna, 'you do that. OK?'

I nodded. Truth to tell, it was a relief to have a reason to take my bruised and hopeful heart away from her, and where better to clear my buzzing brain than up by the clear flowing waters?

FORTY-TWO

Autumn had daubed the trees with gold and dipped the leaves in yellow, crimson and squirrel red. The bracken straggled to tan skeleton curls, and the stream was near icy. But the pool, walled in by towering rocks and the tumbling curtain of the falls, was warm enough to plunge into, though I had to keep swimming rather than floating, for the brilliant sunshine stung with an edge of winter chill. I sat in my shirt, wrung-out jeans stretched on a thorn bush to dry, in the place where I had first met

Rainbow-Wings and seen the butterflies. The air was quiet beyond the roar of the waters.

A riot of blue jays startled me into looking at the opposite shore. They hurtled in and out of the trees' spindly tips like a bunch of rainbowed kites tugged by an impatient child. Something had disturbed them, and I soon saw what, as their bright wings fluttered over the edge of the pool in outraged clamour. A purposeful little clutch of musk-hogs trotted onto the shore, tails whisking, noses shovelling into the sand, stopping suddenly; then off they'd go, straight ahead again. Something about a musk-hog makes me smile: there is no other creature looks so absorbed and busy about doing damn all. Well, I guess there are squirrels, but somehow the way they fly from tree to tree makes it look like an aerial game of chase, where a solid little musk-hog standing still seems made from this earth and rooted there.

I lost myself watching them, and when they doodled back into the undergrowth, I wanted to call out and follow them.

But a grown woman cannot grovel around under the trees for pig nuts and beetles without calling undue attention to herself. She has to walk this earth upright on her own two feet and do whatever she wants to do. And when she can't do what she wants, which, I reminded myself bitterly, is be loved by Suzanna LaReine, she's just got to do – something else.

A huge tattered cloud drew over the sun. I stood up and pulled on stiff jeans and boots, and strolled around the shore with my hands shoved deep in my pockets. I looked up. Listened. No sign of butterflies. The cloud hung motionless in the sky and I worked my sombre way downstream, past the shivering tatters of redbud and bleached black-eyed susans.

Now, maybe I should not have gone to the waterfall that day.

Maybe.

But would it have made a hound's curse of a difference if I'd been at the house?

For while I was away, there had been a mighty dust cloud come helling along from the west and startled everybody to battle positions. Lucille had improvised a sling and hurled a barrage of her odd objects at the intruder. A snaking rawhide whip had caught them like a happy horntoad in a swarm of flies. On the butt end of this whip was a hand hard as steel, a grin that gleamed below eyes of tawny wildfire, and Mary Maloof had tottered upright, swearing her drinkin' and cussin' days were done, her sinnin' was over, for here was an answer to her prayer:

Calamity Jane!

I came back at dusk to find the raunchy, raw-boned Champion Swearer of the Plains in a pool of light on the porch, Suzanna lounging on a post beside her, and everyone else in a circle at her feet. Her voice was rich with rasping humour and as I got near I could hear the flow and pause of a born raconteuse. The kind who'll tell you a tale of an Indian tracker can trail a man from shadow prints on a rock, and another tale of snakes you can hypnotize reciting them poetry, and you're proud to believe every lying word. The whole crew was transfixed, no one more than Suzanna.

'Hey, Typewriter,' said Rainbow-Wings, leaping to her feet. 'What happened?'

'No sign,' I said. 'I saw a bunch of blue jays, some musk-hogs . . . nothing else.'

'Never mind,' said Rainbow-Wings. 'Maybe tomorrow.'

'This here's Calamity Jane!' wheezed Mary Maloof. 'We got ourself one eddicated bitch here, Calam, used ta work the newspapers!'

'I used to sell my life story to newspaper folks,' said Calamity Jane, twinkly and throwing out one big hand. 'Never believe what yuh read on a news-sheet, 's what I say! Pleased tuh meet yuh – you got name other than Typewriter?'

'Suits me,' I said. Something about her made me a shade uneasy.

'Waaall, girls,' said Calamity Jane, 'sundown calls for a drink, hey?'

She talked so easy and sat so easy, like she belonged here. Like she owned the place. Suzanna grinned and fetched a bottle of bourbon.

'Fuck me side to side and backwards too!' Calam shot to her feet. 'Whar the hell's mah memory! I got a dang letter fer somebody here!'

She scooped a folded envelope from her butt pocket.

'Didn't figger on bein' mail rider with no coach,' she said, smoothing out the envelope. 'Who the dadblasted Jesus is Helena Stanforth?'

I held out my hand.

'So that's yer name!' she crowed and thumped my arm. 'Kinda fancy handle, huh?'

I took the letter and slit it open with my thumbnail.

'What's it say?'

I looked up at Suzanna. Couldn't resist it. 'Give me a moment,' I said.

Her eyes didn't even flicker.

FORTY-THREE

Well, Miss Isabella Bird had sure done some fancy stuff. Inside the letter she had folded newspaper clippings exposing van Doon's investment racket in the kind of ice-pick acid-bath English that strips a charlatan to the rotten core. Editorials followed deploring the materialistic corruption of what Old England had hoped would be a Garden of Eden, a New World. Some titled somebody had set up an investigative committee, banks had frozen cheques, and there was a big hoot from Scotland Yard on his way to 'establish the facts'. Van Doon's goose was well and truly cooked by the impeccably wily Miss Isabella Bird.

Her letter read:

My dear Miss Stanforth,

Words alone cannot express the joy I experienced on receiving your letter, albeit filled with such distressing and unpleasant news. I have come across sufficient scoundrels in my peregrinations not to be shocked, more saddened, that such people imagine they can cheat their way through life and hang the consequences! However, I think you will agree, from the newspaper clippings enclosed, that I have not been idle, and, certainly, van Doon and his ilk will have to seek their ill-gotten gains from other shores than these. I was delighted to be invited 'way out west' again, and have to confess that the years have done little to 'cure' my wanderlust, which I never regarded as an illness, more a blessing.

I shall be visiting America – following in the steps of this letter. My only concession to age is allowing myself to travel more comfortably, but this also means more slowly. I have a strong yen to return to the Rockies, but will contact you again when my plans are clear.

I was amazed to read that Helena Stanforth had settled herself more than a hundred yards from the inky delights of a printing press! Do tell me what drew you to your western fastness – more important, what *keeps* you there!

With all good wishes,
    Isabella Bird.

I smiled and handed the package to Suzanna. My doves had come home as vultures!

'Shit, that's good!' she said, grinning straight at me. 'Looks like van Doon got his dang dragon's teeth drawn here!'

She read the letter to the crew, and we toasted the lovely Isabella with a throat-burning shot.

Calamity Jane rose to her feet. She stood near as tall as Suzanna.

'I ain't got no wish tuh be no Cassandry, folks,' she said, looking round us, 'but what I seen this very day in that hickory hole rats' nest back there – Swallering Gulch – your boy don't aim to take no paper warnin'. Hell, he's trainin' up anythin' kin be pinned upright on the back of a cayuse! Givin' 'em rifles and enough shot to git a buffalo shittin'! He's gettin' his money some place else, else my name ain't Calamity! We got tuh git ourselves organized, girls!'

We were all looking to Suzanna to slap her down a little. Like she always did with anything too uppity. But all she did was pass the bottle round and nod.

'We got a few plans,' she said. 'Only we don't carry more than a dozen rifles.'

'Them buzzards gonna claw yuh outta here, fer sure,' said Calamity. 'I seen it! Van Doon's madder en a hornet's nest bin lit with tar paper! But I got a few ideas ridin' in here. You do got an advantage with the pass bein' so narrow and the boy's plannin' to strike in two weeks. Which gives y' a bit of time to git ready . . .'

And so she went on, you'd think none of us had an eye in her head or a brain cell to rub along beside it. And what happened when she'd finished expressing her one-day expert's opinions?

'You're right,' said Suzanna. 'You've got the whole picture, Calam. We have quite some plans for this boy. Come on in and I'll fill you in before supper. You coming, Fingerbone?'

'Yup, sirree!' said Mary Maloof, and the three left us all sitting on the porch struck dumber than if a hurricane had hit.

FORTY-FOUR

It was Rainbow-Wings who spoke first.

'I'm going to have a gander at the night air, you coming? Neta? Amelia?'

Lucille went with them.

Grievous and the twins shifted off to clean up: the three were streaked with sweat and grime like miners.

Which left me and Roo and Mira paying our slow respects to good corn whiskey. I folded Isabella Bird's letter carefully into my pocket. The brash bushwhacking voice of Calamity Jane rang in my ears.

'Ho hum,' said Roo, stirring dust with her toe. Mira shrugged and looked my way.

'Come on down to the bunkhouse,' she said. 'It's getting cold up here. I have some gold tequila with a kiss like fire.'

'You're privileged,' said Roo, with mock injury, as we walked through the cool darkness. 'I've been on at her to open that baby for months.'

'Good thing we didn't,' said Mira, putting a match to the oil-lamp in the bunkhouse. 'It wouldn't have lasted more than five minutes. I have the feeling now's the time. Sit down, Helena – you want to be Helena?'

Right at that moment I wanted to be anybody but. I shrugged. 'Rainbow-Wings called me Fools Rush In,' I said. 'It was Grievous called me Typewriter. Feel like I've worn out every name I've ever used. I could do with a new name altogether.'

Mira broke the seal on the bottle and sat down. Roo put three squat glasses in front of us. Mira sliced a lime and poured a handful of salt into a bowl, tossing the dust over her shoulder.

'You did it, didn't you, Typewriter? I warned you, but you went ahead and did it,' she said sadly. 'You went straight ahead and fell head over heels with Suzanna. And you told her? First?'

I looked at her. Shrugged. 'Guess it was too late when you spoke to me, Mira,' I said. 'Guess I've earned the name Fools Rush In.'

'Don't beat yourself up about it,' said Mira. 'I know she's your angel right now, but the path of love is one Suzanna fears to tread. Honey, she ain't never been able to let herself just take a chance and go for it.'

'It's true,' said Roo. 'Every time someone turns up and gets a thing going with her, we all hold our breath, cross our fingers and pray! Maybe this time? Don't make a spit of difference. Don't nothing last with Suzanna.'

'Not in the way of love,' said Mira. 'She's so tied up with keeping the outfit going, won't hand over none of it to nobody, don't trust no one else to do it right. I kind of hoped it would be different for you and her, seeing as you both go back such a way.'

'See,' said Roo, 'not a one of us was surprised when Angel turned up and Suzanna appeared to have flipped for her. I mean, look at Angel, jailbait jailbird, a real *bad* girl ain't had the hell knocked outta her, mouthy, pushy, sulky and proud as Satan – we thought, uh-oh, here comes trouble. Trouble's what Suzanna goes for. All her life she's been gunning for trouble. It's what keeps her heart beating. She's more pleased about this van Doon trash than a squerril in spring finally found them nuts it buried last winter. Gives her something familiar to do.'

'You saw how she was when Neta and Amelia turned up?' said Mira. 'Just couldn't stand the idea of there being more than one way to trap a bear. Makes her twitchy, y'see. Woman's never happier than when she's holed up some place, back against the wall and all the odds stacked against her. She's always punched or shot her way out of trouble. She don't take to new ways too good.'

I tossed back the tequila. It was good to be with these two strong women, it was even good to hear that maybe the sudden ice age between me and Suzanna wasn't caused entirely by what I'd said or done. Roo refilled our glasses.

'I was thinking of moving on,' I said.

'Uh-huh,' said Roo. 'No one could blame you. We'd all miss you.'

'Trouble is,' I said, 'if I stick around. I guess you get over it some time. Hell, I know you do. But when? When does the day dawn I don't give a shit?'

'And now there's Calam, too,' said Mira. 'I figure you felt the same as us – Suzanna's gone wide-eyed again over another real live outlaw.'

'That fast?' I said. 'Hell, the woman only rode in today.'

'That's Suzanna,' said Roo. 'And don't we all love her? I'm just glad I never flipped for her. Aside from Mira cutting out my guts for a washing line if I had a done, I've seen a lot of good women walking round here with the blues right up to their necks and all for love of Suzanna.'

'She said give it time,' I said, clutching at that golden straw.

'And she meant it,' said Mira. 'There's no lying ways nor tricks to Suzanna. Only what did she mean by time? Could have been a week, a month, a year. Could be the hours and minutes till Calam rode in.'

I put my head on the table. Hell, who was I kidding? 'Give me time' is just a kind-sounding way of saying no. We were through, Suzanna and me, through before we'd even begun. And my damned anguished heart should have known better than to speak to her. She'd dished it out, all right. Now it was up to me how I took it.

I sat up. 'Gimme some more tequila,' I said, forcing my voice to some strength. 'Let's drink to Fools Rush In.'

We clinked glasses and commenced to wiping out the rest of the pale-gold cactus juice.

FORTY-FIVE

Supper at the big house, and me and the girls troll-loll-lolled up the hill, mood courtesy of a broken heart well seasoned with magic, Mexico and mescal.

'Where the hell have you all been?' demanded Suzanna, pacing the living room alone.

'We reckoned you were occupied,' said Roo easily.

Suzanna scowled. 'Just listen,' she said, jerking her thumb at the study door.

We listened. The words weren't clear, but one voice belonged to Calamity Jane, and the hoarse cackles could only come from the throat of Mary Maloof Fingerbone.

'Shit!' snapped Suzanna. 'All evening I've been hearing the life and times of two old buzzards ought to bin certified years back. Well, Mary Maloof anyways. Now her goddamn heroine has arrived, them lips got a new lease of life and spouting off about every damn time and place she's gotten more stewed than anybody else in the history of the universe. So Calam has to top that, every time: if either one of them had drunk a third of what they're bragging about, they'd a bin dead years ago.'

'I thought Fingerbone said Calam had died in her arms?' said Mira.

'Well, she's now testifying to that being the best night she ever had, and Calam don't appear to be able to throw no light on the matter,' said Suzanna, lighting a cheroot. 'Makes me feel I've lived my life like a nun and done nothing, listening to them two. Have a drink.'

'Do you got any tequila?' said Mira. 'I've heard a lady never mixes her drinks.'

Suzanna laughed. 'I was wondering where those three seraphic smiles hailed from,' she said. 'I'll go into the cellar and dig around some.'

Mira nudged me. 'Go with her,' she hissed. 'Grab her! She's mad as hell right now, real put out seeing she ain't centre stage.'

I floated down the cellar steps. She stood, radiant in candlelight.

'You want a hand, Suzanna?' I said, sliding my arm round her shoulders. 'You got mine any time you care for.'

She hugged me fiercely. Put her finger on my lips. 'No words,' she said. 'Just hold me tight. Tight.'

Well, I was tight as a fine lady's asshole, and I held her head to toe. May I die this instant, I thought, delirious at the heaven-sent touch of her neck on my lips, her hair on my cheek.

'Air y'all gittin' some fresh liquor or do we got to piss in a empty bottle fer somethin' tuh drink?'

It was Fingerbone cackling down the stairs. We moved apart slowly.

'Tequila,' said Suzanna, peering into the blackness. 'Bourbon. Catch a hold of this, Typewriter.'

I clutched a square bottle to my chest, in agony and ecstasy. No one could hold me that close unless . . . *You're drunk, you're drunk, you're drunk and in love*, I told myself, for all the good it might do.

All my hopes were dashed when we got back upstairs. Calam was sprawled easy on the chesterfield, Mary Maloof beside her, and Roo and Mira sharing a big leather chair. Suzanna plonked the bottles down and sat facing her outlaw fascination, her eyes all lit up like catherine wheels.

'Well, girls,' said Calam, laying back and stretching her arms out, 'Me and Mary Maloof done *some* talkin'! Yes sirree! How the old days do come back! But we got us a solution, me and Mary Maloof – Suzanna, you aiming to pour that bourbon or use the bottle for a fancy decoration?'

You'd have thought Suzanna was the hired girl as she leaped to obey. I leaned back on Roo's knees and watched her. Yes, I still loved her, for all the difference it didn't make.

'Yup!' said Calam. 'We're headin' out fer Deadwood. Time I saw the old place agin! Besides, girls, there's deeds lodged in a strongbox there kin prove this valley is part and parcel belongin' to one Suzanna LaReine, our good hostess!'

So that was Mary Maloof's secret! But what made Calam imagine that van Doon would take a snip of notice of documentation, when she'd poured scorn on the letter from Isabella Bird? My memory clicked on automatic through the tequila haze. Deadwood . . . Deadwood? It eluded me.

'So these deeds prove beyond a shadder of doubt this place is yours, Suzanna!' crowed Mary Maloof. 'Yuh would never listen to me, would yuh? But yuh'll listen to Calam! Ain't a person breathin' wouldn't pin they ears back when she talks!'

Suzanna looked from one to the other.

'You did that for *me*, y' ole crowspit?' she said, and hugged them both, first Fingerbone, then Calamity Jane, with a warmth whose memory stabbed through me. I remembered that unique warmth in every cell of my body. From the cellar, from the rainbow waterfall, from all my hopes and dreams. From our bed. While I watched and burned, my memory clicked a headline: DEADWOOD. There had been a big arson attack on the deeds office some years back. I couldn't recall the details – it was way out of my patch – but I wondered with dread when Mary Maloof had lodged the deeds.

'Yuh recall when I'm sayin' to yuh, less go west, Suzanna?' wheezed Fingerbone. 'Thass why! And I nevvuh tell yuh, bein' as yuh cut up so ornery evvah time I say the word Deadwood. I provide fer yuh, yaaass I do! All them years ago, I could see yuh're needin' a place tuh be left alone. So I done it! Yuh think I gamble away all mah share of that last bank job? Do I hell! It's yours, Suzanna, writ down and legal.'

'Don't know what to say,' mumbled Suzanna, 'except, thank you, Mother Mary. Seems like we're gonna win this one, hey, girls?'

I had to speak.

FORTY-SIX

I stood up.

'Speaking as a newspaper hack,' I started, putting my hand on my heart, 'I do recall an item of news some years back which may have a cataclysmic bearing on the matter under dishcussion.'

'Why the hail yuh talkin' suh fancy, Typewriter?' said Grievous, astonished.

'Because, my dear GBH, Grievous, my dear, because for a very good reason,' I said, swaying to face her, 'because I am drunk as a shkunk – goddamit! – shk . . . mushk-hog. While my brain can see everything a whole heap clearer thisss way, I have this problem with my wordsh. Shhhit! Words! Articulation! The esses are beginning to go. However, let me continue.'

I took another drink by way of lubrication. Caught Suzanna's eye and allowed myself a gracious bow.

'This here news item pertained to the burning-down of certain offices in Deadwood. Deeds offices. Suspected arson. Damn! I din' think I could shay that! I said it! So, Calam, you and Mary Maloof may take the equessstrian route off into the sssunset and find yourssssselves returning empty-handed, cuz there won't be no deeds there. Maybe.'

I slid to a dignified sitting position on the floor.

'Arson! In Deadwood! *Never!*' Calam was on her feet.

'Them offices been built outta solid stone with lead-lined vaults besides! Built to endoor any kind of attack!'

The words of the report came clear in my mind. I scrambled upright, which I want you to know was a real effort on my part, and spoke:

'"The intense heat of the firebomb attack melted the vaults to a solid lava of metal. The marshal suspects that there is a state-wide organization behind this felony, eager to evict canny ten-cent settlers from rich pasture now worth hundreds of dollars per acre".'

'That what it said?' Calam demanded, thrusting her jaw out.

'To the letter,' I said. 'My memory never lets me down.' I slid to the floor again, now using Grievous's legs as a back rest.

'Like I said, you can't believe a plaguey word them newsfolk print,' bragged Calam. 'Hell, coulda bin a cigarette burned a hole in the fancy carpet and blowed up outta all truth and recognition time it hit the presses! I swear on my whip handle I *know* Deadwood'll provide the way outta this combobulation!'

'I always say so!' seconded Mary Maloof.

'Hope you're right,' I said from the floor. 'Only what makes you think suck-ass van Doon's going to take a sheep's fart of notice of deeds or writsh or any-dam-thing *legal* when he's planning a full-scale invasion? Like you said, Calam, he don't seem to be the boy gives the time of day to legal nothing. We got a boy cornered here and preparing to break every law in the Union to get his way.'

'I'll get a goddam writ on him, or my name ain't Calamity Jane!' she swore, pouring bourbon like it was going out of fashion.

'*Salute! Bonne chance! Venceremos!* Good luck! Mud in your eye! No shit, I hope it works,' I said carefully. The room had become elastic, the floor swaying like a boat in midocean. It stopped if I closed my eyes. From the blessed dark I said, 'I prefer to rely on mud, missiles and tripwires. Catch this fox, you gotta set traps he's never seen before. Get him by all four legs and the tail too!'

Well, I seem to recall a feeling of strong arms under me, but nothing I could be sure of till I woke to what seemed to be morning light. The one blessing of a night on the town with Lady Tequila is she doesn't give you the sledgehammer hangover most other strong liquors feel obliged to mule-kick into you by way of good morning. I noticed a few fresh bruises on my legs and arms: the kind you get walking into doorways and falling up or down stairs. Hmm.

Downstairs was empty, save for Grits in the kitchen scowling at three cauldrons on the range, lids rattling out clouds of steam like a locomotive pulling out of a station.

'Waaall, string me up as a gunney if it ain't Lola Montez!' cackled Grits. 'I swear there was sparks flyin' offa that floor lass night when yuh commenced tuh dancin!' Yuh lookin' white as a sheet, sugar, set down and git this coffee inside yuh!'

'I was dancing?'

'Dancin' like a dervish, playin' the fiddle like a fiend outta hell, and singin'? Yuh have a real paarrful voice fer an eddicated gal!'

That's the only trouble with Lady Tequila. You have a good time, the best time. Everybody tells you for days after what a good time you had, and you can't remember a thing about it, just look at your bruises and everybody's grins and wonder.

'I was singing, Grits?'

'Yuh done some a them ole ballads brought tears tuh my eyes.'

'Oh.'

Grievous came in and grinned as she saw me. 'Danged if it ain't Lotta Crabtree! Yuh got a voice like a nightingale, Typewriter!'

'I have?'

'Yuh know yuh have! What was that song when yuh got the geetar and wuz serenadin' Suzanna?'

Oh, shit.

'I was serenading Suzanna?'

'Yuh sure was! When she wuz up in the balcony, and yuh said it was real Shesspeerian? Blamed if I understood a word of it, but you sure was having a good time!'

'What did Suzanna do?'

'Hell, she was singing along with yuh! A real doo-ett!'

'Hev some more coffee, Typewriter,' said Grits soothingly. 'Keep yuh voice down, Grievous, our songbird's feelin' fragile this morning.'

What all else had I done or said? No doubt I'd get told as the day went by.

FORTY-SEVEN

'What happened to Calam?' I said as the coffee brought warmth and a dull ache to my body.

'She lit outta here at sunup with Mary Maloof. Swears she'll git documentation against van Doon.'

'Hope to hell she's right. Did I tell her about the fire?'

'Bout a dozen times,' said Grievous cheerfully. 'But she wouldn't pay yuh no never-mind, said news hounds was a pack of fools or liars. Yuh don't remember that neither?'

'No.'

'Oh, dear sweet Jesus and the angels! Yuh challenged her tuh a duel, Typewriter.'

'I did?'

'Yuh did! Damn! Yuh stood there and said, clear as a bell, *Calamity Jane, I got nothin' but respect for yuh! But I have a repeetation tuh protect! Choose yuh weapons an' name yuh place!* On'y then yuh went kinda white and pitched flat on yuh face. Kinda spoiled it. Wuz me and Suzanna put yuh tuh baid, honey. Yuh was a deadweight.'

'Oh, hell,' I said. 'Thanks anyway.' Me and my mouth only truly come together when I'm drunk, and even then the mouth has a way of masking what I really want to say. Even drunk I'm a goddam coward. So I'd got into the passionate-defence-of-newspapers jag, had I? I knew that safe script all too well. I went outside and down to where Rainbow-Wings, Lucille, Neta and Amelia were grouped around the plane, great piles of *things* heaped beside them.

'Well, good morning!' said Lucille with her wide gold-gleaming grin. 'If it ain't the juggling act!'

'Juggling?' I said. Surely not.

'Too bloody right!' said Rainbow-Wings. 'All the best fancy crystal and never dropped one glass.'

'That was some party!' said Neta. 'Some cabaret!'

'You don't look too well,' said Amelia. 'Do you want to come up for a spin? It'll either put you right or totally wipe you out.'

'Yes,' I said.

I hadn't been up in the aeroplane yet. Felt a little nervous, tell the truth. But my head was already floating well above the ground: maybe I'd catch hold of it on the way up. I climbed into the big bird and Amelia strapped me in. God knows I have dreamed of flying often enough, and woken up in tears at my slow earthbound body. The musk-hog reality of dawn. When Grievous went up first, I had tried to imagine what it would be like with the ground just dropping away . . . As the plane bumped along I braced my feet on the floor and then we took off.

It was smooth, with everything so neat and small from the air. Neta, Rainbow-Wings and Lucille were dolls on a green velvet cloth. Trees were twigs, the house was a matchbox, and as we swung over it, I saw a tiny blonde figure shading her eyes to look up at us. Suzanna! What else had I said or done last night? I felt apprehensive.

'*Where?*' mouthed Amelia. I pointed south, and the plane swooped across the valley swifter and truer than an arrow. I looked down at the wild horses and their proud stallion flinging his head up as we passed overhead. Then we were above the first straggling belt of trees on the foothills, dashed over the stone-signed saddle Suzanna and I had sweated and ached to find . . . I motioned Amelia to circle, until we were over the strange red-stone chess-game valley. This is how a giant would see it: an outcrop no bigger than a pincushion. I was glad to remember the time I'd spent there with Suzanna. It meant something I couldn't put into words, it was precious to me.

'*Where now?*' mouthed Amelia. I smiled and shrugged. I'd seen what I wanted to. The plane wheeled out over the valley and we scudded towards the western pass, circling when we caught sight of Grievous and the twins and their intricate zigzag of trenches. We coasted down, almost shaving the top of their heads. They leaped up and down, whooping and waving their hats. Amelia smiled and took us higher until they were little more than dots. We cleared the western pass, and went still higher, blinded for a moment by cloud. Through the white gusts, the barren plain below, littered with bleached-timber pin-sized derelict buildings.

'*Hold on!*' Amelia howled, and cut the engine's roar. In the sudden silence, she said, 'We'll coast over Swallering Gulch and I'll take her right back up after. See what you can see!'

Well, what was there to see? A dusty main street with a couple of alleys trickling off it . . . and a corral lined on three sides with dark ant shapes, tiny puffs of smoke: van Doon's firing range, van Doon's army. I picked out a teensy surrey white as the devil's spit on brambles in the autumn. A blonde head, a dark head, and a parasol.

'Seen enough?' said Amelia.

I nodded wordlessly. The engine screamed us deaf and we soared above the cloud, where Swallering Gulch

170

looked like a broken muddied trinket scattered on the ground.

FORTY-EIGHT

The flight had blown my blues away: seeing Swallering Gulch, where van Doon was making his preparations, from such a height put me in mind of a word Spanish women and men use in a wholly different way.

Macho.

The men cannot say it without puffing their chests out and tightening their hips and calf muscles. Noble, brooding, powerful, adorable *hombres machos!*

But the women! Take the *ch* in macho and say the whole word like you were spitting out chewing tobacco gone stale, and you have it. Empty strutting, blood-and-thunder, spit-worthy, pain-in-the-ass. *Macho.*

And that was van Doon and his minions. I wondered how Mercedes was squaring her feelings about macho men now she was working with them; more, I wondered how Angel was feeling, betraying her natural mother into those cruel, greedy hands. And how were the pair of them getting along with sweet Lulumae, Daddy's little girl? The picture held a certain grim amusement. I'd have loved to be a fly on the wall over dinner.

I sat back and enjoyed the sweep of evening sunshine over the valley. We bumped along the ground and landed.

'Thank you, Amelia,' I said and squeezed her hand.

'No sweat,' she said. 'You're looking better, too.'

I swung to the ground. Felt a bit like hitting land the first time I ever got off a boat, only this time I felt small, like the air was weighting me down.

'Just back in time for supper!' said Lucille, with her lazy smile. We strolled to the house.

Suzanna sat at the head of the table and nodded us in.

171

The meal ran in silence beyond 'Hiya' and smiles, until she spoke.

'Well, Calam and Fingerbone have hit the trail. Aiming to be back in two, three days. If they don't stumble across too many bars,' she said drily. She was back on her lonely high horse, proud and lovely, and exuded an unquestionable authority. She looked around at us all, and her storm-cloud eyes met mine for a second, setting my heart racing.

A perverse glimmer of hope sprang alive like a firefly: maybe she'd changed her mind, maybe I'd read her all wrong, maybe there was an *us* to be enjoyed, after all. All my maybes sparked to life, ghost gold in the dark fields of my mind. For all I goaded myself away from *once upon a time*, scorning the unlikelihood of *they lived happily ever after*, somewhere I hoped, believed, that this once-in-a-lifetime dream would come true.

Rainbow-Wings waited until everyone had given an update on their work. Then she beckoned us into the lounge and sat cross-legged on the floor. Never had her green eyes burned so dark: where they were dancing with the promise of spring leaves when I first met her, now they held the olive of winter firs, where breezes and chill sunlight toss around every green there is. As she spoke, her eyes danced jade, moss, emerald, high-sea green, sea-thistle blue, green of brilliant plumage, the secret green of dusty lush ivy.

'We've done what we know,' she said. 'And I have a story to tell all of you, dear women, my friends, my lovers.'

Amelia and Neta looked at each other, surprised. *You, too?* Yes, all of us in the room had shared that wordless ecstasy with Rainbow-Wings, been taken away from our loneliness, taken closer to ourselves in her arms. And we all knew. And Lucille, closer to her than any of us, gave her gleam-of-gold smile and welcomed us.

'The circle is closing,' said Rainbow-Wings. 'It is the way it was when the white men came first and my people were scattered to the four winds by the vile triangle of Greed, Disease and Murder. But now there is a four again. Kimama has four sides, and the rocks hold us safe on three. This is the third season, the season of danger, and soon the fourth season will come to save us and drive our enemies away with frost and snow. We have harnessed the four powers: earth and what lies beneath the earth, Grievous and the magic of twins; the sky is ours, we have *Vega* to dazzle them with, Amelia and Neta; what lies in the ocean is ours, for the waters flow to confound them; and fire is ours, Suzanna.

'This is the way it will be,' she went on in the charmed firelight. 'No need for fear. Let the fear be theirs. For they will ride in on horses driven by spurs and whips. They will ride in, heavy with guns and shot, mouths bragging and drinking, prepared to snuff out the silly light of a dozen women. Through the pass they will be brave, and then the roaring in the sky will terrify them as they look up and stumble and fall into the covered mouths of earth. Let the fear be theirs.'

'You know what Rainbow-Wings said to me when I first got here?' said Suzanna gruffly, when we were alone. 'I said I didn't know what I was doing, taking on this whole valley. She laughed like a strong woman ridin' high on smoke or liquor and said the valley had taken me on. That it would be here when I was long gone. Feels that way now. Feels like I'm just the hired girl – feels like it's all out of my hands. I get kind of hypnotized listening to her, then when she's gone I think and I can't get a word of sense out of my thoughts.'

I looked at her tortured face. Fought the urge to smooth out the worry with my lips or fingertips.

'I'd be a heap happier if we had a goddam arsenal here!' she exploded, turning to me. 'Do you know what I mean?'

'These are strange times,' I said. 'Guess we all have to find new ways to do things.'

She was miles away. 'Y'see, when Calam rode in, I felt so strong again,' she said. 'That's one woman knows what she's about.' She pursed her lips and ripped a match along her boot-heel. 'And then there's Angel,' she said. 'Some day I'm going to have to face that child of mine, and right now all I want to do is shake the little bastard to shit! And Mercedes! When I think what we did to get her here! Her and her goddam stiletto!'

And then there's me, too, I thought heavily, the one with the ragged heart on her sleeve. Suzanna brooded into the fire, all her cares giving a sag to those wonderful shoulders, a furrow to her brow.

'I dunno, dunno, dunno, dunno!' she said finally.

I put a mask on my mouth. It had got me into enough trouble already. I saw her so crystal clear, I felt, and then she would turn a little and another dazzling facet would hit me, and I'd start all over again, trying to make sense of her, trying to make sense of the elusive tantalizing rainbow light playing from the heart of her.

'Let's sleep,' she said.

We slept. A little uneasy, but close.

FORTY-NINE

By the end of the week, we were ready. Each day, Amelia took *Vega* on a dawn patrol over the pass. Grievous and the twins spiked their tripwires with dynamite; we all had woven flimsy mats of branches to cover the pits and spread earth over them. There was a wide swampy belt of dark mud no horse could ride through, and when the fools saw that, they'd have to spread out, and make a real target of themselves.

Tuesday Calam and Mary Maloof came helling back, burst into the house around suppertime. Suzanna lit up at the sight of them, her eyes went to Calam's face with a telltale blush. In a voice a sight more nervous than you'd expect to come from her, she said, 'Well?'

'Well, we bin to Deadwood,' said Calam, oblivious to it all. 'I swear I wouldn't know the place! Not a body on the streets as knew me neither. And you were right, newspaper lady. Not a shred of documentation survived that fire. But I did find out one thing: the finger's out for Darknell van Doon. Seems the boy's dadblamed nifty with fire-raising, and never to be found within fifty miles.'

'Figures,' I said, and told her about Chicago.

'So that wasn't an entire waste of time,' said Calam.

'And sumpin else besides,' burst out Fingerbone. 'Fa Gawd's sake gimme a drink – tell 'em, Calam!'

'Waaall,' said Calam with a smile. 'This is how it went . . .'

Seems both her and Fingerbone had gotten more than a mite depressed in Deadwood. All the bars were fancied up, and filled with dudes looked sideways at two bushwhackin' old-timers out to burn their brains. They'd lurched from one saloon to the next, and no amount of liquor would raise their spirits. They'd saddled up and left before dawn, and devised a plan in the rosy glow of sunrise.

Figuring van Doon wouldn't associate Calam with Suzanna, and wouldn't recognize Fingerbone upright on a horse as the sprig-muslined needle-clackin' granmaw he'd met here, they rode into Swallering Gulch and sat around in the hotel there, eyes alert and ears flapping like shingleboard roofs in a twister. They'd made a point of sitting at the next table to van Doon, Lulumae, Mercedes and Angel. Mercedes didn't notice them, being as she was busy making sheep's eyes at van Doon and he was doing his best to make 'em right back without Lulumae cottoning on.

'Waaall,' cackled Fingerbone, 'Angel noticed me straight off, and I could see her thinkin', Is it, ain't it? On'y she's never clapped eyes on me sober. Sheeee-it! If thet ride to

Deadwood din' take years offa me! You tell 'em the rest, Calam.'

'We sat around in the bar afterwards, and then that petticoated rattlesnake took herself off to bed in a huff if ever I seen one. Yer boy starts gettin' real serious 'bout his bulgin' eyes once she's gone, and yer little cactus flower's shinin' bright as the noonday sun. So I see yer child, Suzanna, and she looks like she's chewin' on somethin' sour where she was expectin' a sugar lump and don't rightly know how to spit it out. We wait. Shortly, van Doon and – whass her name? – Assassina, they go out to take the night air. Hah! Never seen the like, a goddam boa constrictor arm in arm with a coyote, steppin' out fer a promenade! Which leaves Angel on her own, lookin' our way and pretendin' she ain't. I go over to her and buy her a drink. She sure is glad!'

'Even glad to see *me*!' cackled Fingerbone. 'Seems she's got herself a conscience and don't like what it's tellin' her! You tell 'em, Calam!'

'Waaall, me and Angel git to talkin', and Mary Maloof finally decides she's poisoned her gut enough for one day. We don't say nothing about what's goin' on here, and me and Angel, well, we spend the night talkin'. Seems like she do think a whole heap of her momma, after all, and she'd do anythin' to git back here. 'Sides, she knows ever'thin' there is to know about ole Darknell. Boy don't stand a chance!'

'What about Angel?' Suzanna broke in, intensely.

'I'm back,' said a voice from the doorway. Angel Star, looking like she'd been whupped, mighty pale and worried about could she put a toe over the doorway without it would get shot off.

'C'mon in, honey,' said Calam. 'Yer riding with me.'

Angel looked only at Suzanna. They both had the kind of gaze that would send smoke and flame curling off wood. Neither wavered, but Angel moved forwards as if in a trance.

'I'm eatin' that mile of dirt right now, Suzanna,' she said. 'Will you have me back?'

Suzanna held out her arms and held Angel close.

'Thank Christ!' said Angel on a sob. 'I was sure I'd made a mistake soon as I rode into Swallering Gulch! I'd do anything to make it better!'

'Told yuh it'd be fine, honey, din' I?' said Calam, slinging an arm round Angel protectively. The younger woman turned to her and buried her head on Calam's shoulder.

'C'mon, I don' ride with no bitches goin' soft on me!' protested Calam. She kissed Angel full and firm on the lips and squeezed her hand.

'Gawd, I love you, Calam,' said Angel. 'And I love you, Suzanna. I'm so glad I met you, Calam, else I'd have lost my own mother!'

Suzanna's face was a study. 'So, I've got me a daughter again,' she said huskily. 'Best if we drink to that! Come right on in!'

Yes, Suzanna had a daughter again. A prodigal daughter who'd ridden back on the arm of Calamity Jane, and the way Suzanna felt about that tawny outlaw, she'd have welcomed a vulture as a house pet, if Calam said so. Not that she wasn't pleased to have Angel back. But our late-night conversation was terse and sombre.

'Y'see, Typewriter, I was getting mighty fond of Calam.'

'I've got eyes in my head,' I told her.

'You *knew*?' she said, startled.

'I knew. It's written all over your face, Suzanna, and I have to admit I spend a lot of time reading your face.'

'That's why I didn't say anything to you, and it hurt, cuz I feel I can tell you anything. It just don't seem fair. Why the hell don't things ever fit together? Why don't I love you? Why does Calam go for my daughter and not me?'

She'd said it. I drained my glass.

'That's life, Suzanna,' I said bitterly. 'A one-eyed bitch

dealing from a crooked pack. You get the queen of hearts, and I get the joker.'

'I – ' she began, but I cut her short.

'Let's leave it,' I said, rising to go to bed. 'Maybe, hell, maybe nothing. No point in talking about it, I've had it with words.'

I walked upstairs, torn between turning back to where she sat alone in the firelight, flinging myself to my knees beside her. But what for? I loved her and it hurt like hell to know she didn't love me. There was enough to do round here. Stuff like sleeping and keeping busy. But that silver-eyed hag, sleep, passed my door without a pause that night and every night that followed.

FIFTY

We had taken to standing in the kitchen drinking coffee round the range at all hours, twitchy for when van Doon would strike. Angel said he'd start out real early, under the cover of mist, as soon as his supplies of shot, powder and dynamite arrived. He was planning to horseshoe around us and fire oil-soaked rags at the house to burn us out, imagining that we would retreat before such an awesome display of gratuitous *machismo*. Amelia's dawn patrol was sure to spot him.

On the third day, Rainbow-Wings appeared at the door in the darkness before dawn, holding one arm out like an intricately carved candelabra. She demanded silence with her sage-brush eyes, and pointed, whipping long fingers back in an exaggerated *Hush!* Her arm was swathed from shoulder to fingertip in exquisite winged shapes, moth-fragile, and in the heat, they began to rustle. The butter-flies! But, oh, how late, how weary!

Grits unscrewed a honey jar and poured a great scoop across the scrubbed table. The butterflies shivered from

Rainbow-Wings's copper arm and hand and flocked around the sticky pool, antennae quivering.

'The storms they've been through!' breathed Rainbow-Wings. 'There are millions by the falls. They need to be here, to be warm, come!'

The white sun of early winter cast an eerie bleached light as we followed her to the falls. The chill stream pushed icy fingers against our legs. In the cliff shadow by the lake was Lucille, like a wise woman in a feather cape, hordes of butterflies all over her body. Grits handed the gallon jars of honey to Rainbow-Wings, who anointed us with sweetness until all the honey was gone. The sun tipped over the falls and we gasped. For the pool was petalled with dead wings, the shore littered with papery corpses, a landscape of nightmare. But from the trees and bushes came a sigh as the survivors struggled towards us, landing on hair, face, neck, sleeves, shoulders, and we tiptoed back to the house as if we were carrying robins' eggs.

'Where the hell have you been?' cried Amelia, then hushed as we catwalked to the table and our precious cargo crawled and flittered to coat the table, the chairs, the roof beams.

'It's today,' said Rainbow-Wings.

'Yes! They started out from Swallering Gulch over an hour ago. There's at least two hundred of them,' said Amelia.

'Three hundred and forty-seven,' said Angel wearily, 'not counting van Doon and Assassina. And Lulumae. You couldn't get that one to miss out on a bloodbath.'

'So they'll be at the pass shortly after noon,' said Suzanna. 'Time enough.'

There came a ricochet of buckshot: we all stiffened. Fourteen women, and thirteen of us soaked to the knees and drenched with honey from there on up.

'It's the rain!' cried Rainbow-Wings, and led us outside, where late-autumn clouds had split apart. And we danced in the rain, we fell in the rain, we stripped mother-naked as the rain streamed down our bodies.

I knew van Doon and his hirelings would be hunched up and scowling, lips curling curses at the heavens above; I could picture van Doon the fire-raiser confounded in the inundation.

We dried off by the range, speaking in whispers so as not to alarm the exhausted butterflies, and as we dressed by the huge fire Suzanna had lit in the big room, the drum tattoo on the roof eased to drips, and a defiant watery sun threw the whole landscape into pale relief.

FIFTY-ONE

'There they are!'

Amelia's binoculars passed from hand to hand. Van Doon's hirelings poured through the pass like rats from a drain. The first few floundered in the mud, and those behind cannoned into them. One figure in a high white stetson waved its arms, and the pack fanned out and galloped around the mud-wallow.

'Van Doon,' spat Suzanna. 'He's done us a real favour wearing that fancy hat. Makes a fine easy target.'

Chaos and confusion as they hit the covered trenches and hurtled over the horses' heads as we had thought. Grievous and the twins whooped as still more tumbled underground. From the woods came dull explosions and bursts of charred smoke as more met their end on the dynamited tripwires. The little puppet in his white hat rallied the remnants of his army and still they straggled on, maybe a hundred, and fighting mad. More arm-waving from van Doon, I could imagine his bluster: *Ain't but a bunch of women out there, boys! Ef this is the best they can do, we'll wipe 'em out!*

Suzanna nodded at Rainbow-Wings and she and Amelia

took off in *Vega*. The great bird swooped low and Grits hollered:

'Thar goes mah sewin' machine! Shoot! They missed that ole swagger-britches! Let 'em have it, girls!'

Pandemonium on the plain as the horses bolted from the roaring shadow overhead, scattering the paid murderers far and wide. Small puffs of shot gathered in the air, hundreds of feet below the white avenging wings! They were fool enough to think they could shoot *Vega* down!

Still they galloped on, the rat-hirelings whipping their horses to a frenzy. Odd objects rained on them from the sky, hitting a few, terrifying the rest. From the trees, Roo, Calam, Mira and Angel blasted away at the tattered remnants as soon as they were in range: the whole swarming mass of them stopped, yelled curses at van Doon, and for all his bellowing and waving, they wheeled round and hightailed right back where they had come from, leaving him alone. Not quite. There was one figure beside him. Suzanna seized the binoculars.

'Van Doon and Mercedes!' she hissed. 'He's mine!'

We watched him tear the linen from his back and tie a flag of surrender to his rifle. Mercedes's face was twisted with rage – she spat at him.

'I could always talk to Mercedes,' said Grievous, as they drew near. 'She ain't all bad! It's time for words, they got a damn white flag there!'

Before we could stop her, she rushed forwards and yelled, 'Mercedes!'

Van Doon jerked a gleam of metal from his coat and hot lead smacked Grievous's body to the ground.

'*God damn you, Suzanna LaReine!*' he bellowed.

Suzanna stepped forward, bent and touched Grievous's dear, dead cheek. Then she rose to face van Doon and Mercedes, her face alight with a hatred made of steel.

I had my eye on Assassina, sitting on her horse behind van Doon like the angel of death. I knew she'd do something desperate now the chips were down for good

181

and all. As they came up to the house, I saw her sick smile when she saw Grievous's body lying there, a bullet with Suzanna's name on it through her heart. Van Doon's eyes were bloodshot with fear, and his sweaty lips blathered like a crazy person. Stone mad! Incredibly he was still offering *terms*, a loose avalanche of dry-mouthed words tumbling their empty bluff, as if there was still an ace to be pulled out of the bottomless hole he'd dug himself.

'Some people don't know when they're beat.' Suzanna silenced him with deadly scorn. 'You're lucky you're not casting a polkadot shadow alongside your hirelings – get riding, *Mr* van Doon. And don't look back. Killing's too good for you.'

Van Doon's shoulders slumped and his clay feet commenced to crumble under buckled knees. The boy was beat, and he knew it. With a screech, Assassina flicked her wrist and a silver gleam whistled through the air. I flung myself in front of Suzanna, and the stiletto stung me with deadly fire. There was the savage echoing bark of a dozen guns, and Assassina and van Doon stumbled together like the dying winners of a dance marathon, then pitched to the ground. A dozen scarlet roses bloomed a distortion of death through their clothes.

I staggered with the acid pain through my ribs and felt Suzanna's strong arms round me, looked up into her sweet eyes through strands of mist, and tried to hear the words her lips were saying as ghost drums beat loud in my ears.

'. . . be all right, for chrissake, just hang on . . . love you . . .'

My heart rallied for a moment. Long enough for my eyes to clear and focus on the finest woman I'd ever met. Someone seemed to be switching lights out all over the place, and shadows moved in until I could only see her eyes, her storm-grey eyes . . . then nothing.

EPILOGUE

I had given up on riding as the path contoured upwards in switchback swirls. I should be over the pass by noon. Dawn, my mare, picked her way carefully behind me, snorting in the rising heat of the day. We had rested well the night before and risen at sunup. Above us, the peaks were kissed with gold, against a sky of dizzy blue. From the wild whispered rumours that had drawn me this far west, the valley we were headed for held what I'd been looking for all my life. Finally, a place to cool my itchy feet and let the mare run free.

I could hardly wait . . .

OTHER VIRAGO BOOKS OF INTEREST

OUT THE OTHER SIDE

Contemporary Lesbian Writing

Edited by Christian McEwen and Sue O'Sullivan

In *Out the Other Side*, a collection of essays, interviews, speeches and articles, letters and journal entries, all the contributors identify as lesbian – and proudly so! – but the issues covered are by no means exclusive. There is, for example, not a single 'coming out' story. Instead the emphasis rests on the 'other side' of being out. Once a woman defines herself as lesbian, how does it affect all the other choices in her life? How does a lesbian think about sex, about families and children, about race or class or money or work, about incest or alcoholism, health or disability?

Here, more than thirty writers, half of them living in Britain, half in North America, attempt to answer these questions. Among them are: Gloria Anzaldúa, Berta Freistadt, Meiling Jin, Audre Lorde, Siegrid Nielson, Lisa Saffron, Marg Yeo, and many more. Their experiences vary tremendously. But always there is something of a shared tone, an urgency, an engagement. It is the tone of those who know their own situation well enough to reach beyond it, whose wish to describe it is also a decision to act so that ultimately, in Irena Klepfisz's words, 'distances dissolve and differences are nourished'.

NAMING THE WAVES

Contemporary Lesbian Poetry

Edited by Christian McEwen

Love and desire, childhood and children, the value of
sisterhood, self-identity and racism, day-to-day pleasures
and sorrows, the overarching reality of lesbian oppression
– and defiance of that oppression: these are the themes of
this vibrant collection of contemporary lesbian poetry from
both sides of the Atlantic. Here too is a naming and
celebrating of difference in the sense of recognising, giving
form to what was always there. *Naming the Waves* includes
more than 70 poets, both known and unknown: among
them are Mary Dorcey, U.A. Fanthorpe, Irena Klepfisz,
Audre Lorde, Suniti Namjoshi, Adrienne Rich, Sapphire,
Marg Yeo, and many more. In poems that are wonderfully
distinct in form and tone – folksongs, prose poems,
sestinas – are many moods: from the rhythmical lament of
'Waulking Song' to the quietly joyful 'leaves and potatoes',
from the electrifying fear in 'He Touched Me' to the angry
confrontation in 'Some Things about the Politics of Size'.
And behind the wit and feistiness, the tenderness and
anger, lies work in which 'the clear-eyed child and the
outraged adult start to merge', their poems all becoming
part of the same endeavour, the telling of important truths.

BROKEN WORDS

Helen Hodgman

'Helen Hodgman combines acute observation with a surreal imagination to give a stylishly bizarre account of the lives of a group of urban women now: *Broken Words* is funny and poignant, a vivid evocation of the cruelty and beauty of life' – *Shena Mackay*

In this extraordinary novel we discover the seedier sides of Clapham Common life as we meet Moss, her young son Elvis and her lover Hazel, scraping by on the DHSS. Then Moss' ex-husband tips up, pursued by the cult he has abandoned and Hazel's ex, Le Professeur de Judo, begins to think murderously of her back in Vancouver. We meet Walter, too, walking his dog Angst on the Common, and Buster and Beulah from the Women's Design Collective, their offspring a result of the milkman's sperm donation (swapped for a rare Beatles' bootleg). Finally, there is the Bogeyman with his chipped junkie eyes who Elvis shadows, dizzy with love.

As the sun rises and sets beyond the distant towerblocks and snow falls on the Common, the balances of people's lives shift and strain . . .

A bizarre black comedy of contemporary urban life, *Broken Words* is written with sparse elegance and a fierce wit. This, Helen Hodgman's third novel, is a *tour de force*.